SUNRISE OVER MOMBASA

by

Allen Barallon

SUNRISE OVER MOMBASA

First printing 2014

ISBN: 978-0-9942171-0-3

Published by The Mickie Dalton Foundation

Kempsey, NSW

Australia

www.mickiedaltonfoundation.com

Acknowledgement

My Gratitude to my wife for putting up with the long hours of having to listen to the constant alterations to the story.

Many thanks also to my children and their families who, I believe, gave their honest opinions that gave rise to the changes.

About the Author

Allen was born and raised in the Seychelles. He attended school at the Seychelles College and moved to Africa at the age of seventeen,

He stayed and worked in Africa for seven years before moving to Melbourne, Australia late in 1964. But the Melbourne climate did not suit him and he moved to Sydney a year later.

He met and married his wife Yvonne in the mid-1970s. Between them they have four children, three residing in Australia and one in America.

He has travelled throughout Africa, Europe, Asia and America. Fluent in French and English, he also speaks Creole and Swahili.

He now lives in Brisbane where he writes articles for travel magazines and he is also working on two more novels.

The Author

Introduction

The story begins in the early 1950s. Gary is a young man who grew up on a small island in the Indian Ocean that had little communications with the outside world. Shortly before his eighteenth birthday, his father who was separated from his mother and resided in Kenya was declared missing. After finishing school and awaiting results for university placement, Gary decided to travel to Kenya and search for him. His search was put on hold when on his arrival in Africa, he found that a state of emergency had been declared over the whole country and all men of eighteen years and older were automatically drafted in the Kenya Police Regiment to do home guard duties protecting farmers around Nairobi and the Rift Valley for a period of six months. Gary had to defer university.

His adventure took him deep into Mau Mau territory with encounters with both the terrorists and the white farming families of East Africa.

Resuming the search for his Dad at the end of his service, he received news that an acquaintance he met on the ship and became friends with, had his wife and daughter kidnapped by a group of Somalia bandits called the Shiftas. Again he put the search for his father on hold to help with the rescue.

The story tells of the ship travel to Africa, the trip by steam train from Mombasa to Nairobi, the involvement of home guard duties protecting families in the Rift Valley, the life styles of the white settlers, the search around the coastal province, meetings with the Taita and Taveta tribes, their customs and habitat and the Luo tribes of Lake Victoria

Along the way he receives help from the most unlikely people.

Chapter 1

The British East India steam Navigation ship, the (*SS Kampala*) sat motionless outside the entrance into Kilindini Harbour waiting for daybreak and the arrival of a pilot and tug boats to enter the Port. The sun was slowly climbing over the horizon as the ship eventually made its way to the harbour on this sixth day of November, 1953.

The temperature was already in its tropical highs and soaring, with humidity well into the nineties.

Gary's mother had bought him an open return ticket; eight hundred shillings in travelling money and a transfer from Barclays Bank should further funds be required.

Many times while growing up, he had heard his Mother share with him, his sisters, and little brother, the fond memories, stories, history and beauty of this East African Island of Mombasa that is joined to the mainland by a Causeway to the North, a Bridge to the East, and the Likoni Ferry making the Southern crossing. The entire island is completely surrounded by very deep water.

Well before dawn, he was up on deck, showered, casually dressed in a pair of slacks and a light shirt, ready to witness for himself the wonders of Africa, and take

1

several photographs that he would later send home to his Mum.

Along the foreshores of this 500 metres wide entrance, traditional dressed Swahili women in their brightly coloured printed cotton sheets, called the *kanga*, hauling huge loads balanced on their heads, both hands loaded with raffia bags and babies strapped on their backs, while the husbands wearing a type of sarong coloured in bright bands called the *Kikoi*, proudly walking empty handed several paces ahead along the path leading to the Likoni Ferry Terminal, obviously heading to the town market.

On the far side of the entrance were fishers in their dugout canoes busily casting nets, and inspecting traps that had been set and left overnight, and emptying their catches at the bottom of the canoes.

The ferry had stopped, giving priority to ships entering the harbour. Standing on the port side deck watching the ship dock, Gary was approached by a well-dressed man who introduced himself as Anthony Phillips. Through their conversation, he established that Anthony was travelling from India accompanied by his wife and a young daughter to take a new position in Kenya.

The man went on to say that he had observed Gary on several occasions, busily studying a Swahili translation booklet, which he was carrying around like a personal bible, and wanted to know if he was making progress as he would have to learn the language soon.

Gary found him to be very polite, and an interesting person who asked lots of questions with such ease, that before he realised it, he had freely given his reason for coming to East Africa.

2

In the midst of their conversation, Anthony was suddenly called away by an officer from the ship. He excused himself and left.

Gary stood gazing down at the stevedores preparing to embark and unload the ship.

"Mombasa has a unique smell, different from any other places I have ever visited," said an elderly gentleman with a strong European accent standing a few feet away. Gary could not recall having seen him on the ship during the voyage.

"The smell," the man went on to say, "is very hard to describe, a combination of sea, air, humidity, exotic spices and a few other essences giving this place a fragrance of its own."

"Do other East African sea ports have that smell?" Gary asked.

"Entirely different," the man replied. "If you had me blindfolded anywhere else in the world, and somehow beamed me over here, I would know exactly where I was by the smell."

Chapter 2

Gary's parents lived in Kenya until the early 1940s and he was barely five when his mother and father amicably separated.

She moved back to her birth place, the Seychelles, a group of islands about a thousand miles from the East Coast of Africa, taking with her his two sisters, his baby brother and him.

His father stayed in East Africa, kept in close contact and provided financially well for them all. However, soon after Gary's eighteenth birthday in August 1953, all communication suddenly ceased. Although their monthly allowances were still coming, the lack of contact caused great concern.

Worried, his mother contacted friends in East Africa, but they too had not heard from him for several months.

With the Mau Mau uprising, and communication between the two countries limited due to the island possessing no air services, and public telephone services minimal, contacts was mainly by ship that visited twice a month, telegrams in emergencies and radio news broadcasting by the BBC from London once a day in the evening.

The East African authorities with limited personnel did not have the manpower to put up a missing person search, they were told.

Gary's father was the second child born of seven brothers and a sister, originating from a wealthy family also from the Seychelles. He was a very bright young man who graduated from school with honours and was sent to England to study medicine.

However when his father suddenly passed away and failed to leave a will, this caused the family to lose most of their fortune. Through lack of funds his studies were put on hold.

He deferred university and took a job with the British Government in a position that was available with the postal system in the East African state of Tanganyika. He worked extremely hard trying to save enough money to return to university and complete his studies.

Soon after, the Second World War broke out and put another halt to his quest, but he kept working hard and was eventually promoted to Post Master General. He met Gary's mother while on holiday visiting his parents in the Seychelles. They married soon after, started a family and he never went back to complete his studies.

Gary grew up and did all his schooling at the Seychelles College on the main island called Mahe. The college was run under strict rules by the Marist Brothers mostly from Canada. He enjoyed school and was good at most sport, but the activity at which he excelled was Soccer, a popular game that was played then.

They lived away from the main town, although it was a distance of only fifteen miles. The lack of transport, dirt roads and mountainous passes made it extremely difficult to traverse daily, so he stayed at his grandmother's residence in town during the week and went home on weekends.

The Seychelles consist of a group of 115 islands, Mahe being the largest with an area of sixty square miles. Its highest peak reaches 905 metres, with a population of fewer than forty thousand people, seventy per cent residing on Mahe. Being very mountainous, it does not leave a great amount of land for shore activities. A tropical temperature that stays between 26 to 28 degrees all year round, turns the sea into the playground, children learn to swim at a very early age, drowning was rarely heard of. Swimming, fishing, snorkelling and sailing were the main daily activities.

From an early age Gary had the ability to make sound judgement, one of his favourite past time was watching and observing people and their behaviours, by the age of fifteen he had accomplished the art of being able to take control of any unforseen situation that confronted him, to the extent when his friends although much older than him were always seeking his opinion.

He was a very popular and bright student, but a little shy and he detested crowds, but had a great personality, and that of course attracted a lot of friends. He was well-liked by his teachers and respected by his friends and was sexually active in his early teens, attracting ladies a lot older than he was. He was even told by those who detested his popularity that women were not sexually attracted to him, but wanted to mother him. That of course did not worry him a great deal as he was well aware that the few encounters he's had with the opposite sex had so far brought positive result. Of course, that was nothing unusual for the island, as most of people he knew seemed to have high sex drives, either due to the warm weather or the Island diet.

By November that year, after finishing school and awaiting final exam results and University placement due at the end of February the following year, Gary decided that he should take the opportunity to personally go and search for his father. His mother was very apprehensive at first, but with his insistence she decided to let him go, which is why he was on the SS Kampala after a five day journey, entering Kilindini Harbour that morning.

Chapter 3

The Port was extremely busy with the arrival of the Castle Line passenger liner from the UK, which entered the harbour just ahead of them and was given priority. British Troops were being unloaded from the ship by a dozen or so Army transport carriers, making several trips to wherever their barracks were, while more troops were disembarking. Gary estimated that there must have been well over 500 men in that platoon.

As soon as they were docked, he saw Anthony and his family leaving the ship accompanied by two Army officers. Not knowing the cause worried him somewhat, making him wonder whether his new acquaintance was a wanted person or some kind of fugitives, and had been apprehended.

Since the officers escorting him were not showing signs of aggression and eased his mind.

After several hours, passengers from the *SS Kampala,* got the all clear to leave the ship and proceeded through custom. At the counter, Gary handed his passport and immigration papers to the custom officer, and after a quick examination of his entry forms, he was instructed to sit in one of the chairs lined up near an office on the opposite side, where another three young men sat and told to wait. He asked the reason but was told it was normal procedure. Within ten minutes a uniformed army officer called out his name and ushered him into an office where a senior officer sat, a lighted cigarette burning on an ashtray that was filled with cigarette butts, leisurely talking on the telephone and waved him to take a seat.

The officer routinely asked the reason for him visiting Kenya. Gary was surprised by the question, as this was his birth place and automatically made him a citizen of the country, but hoping for a speedy exit, he gave the reason.

He was then informed that due to the uprising in Nairobi, Kenya had been declared a state of emergency. Being a citizen, he automatically qualified to be drafted into the Kenya Police Regiment (KPR). His plea for leniency and the urgency of finding his father was totally ignored by the officer.

Knowing that his plight had fallen on deaf ears, he didn't waste any more time arguing. He was taken to an office complex about half a mile from the Port to await further instruction. The receptionist, a lady in her late thirties was busily concentrating on her typing as they entered and she did not acknowledge their presence for a long time. Gary estimated it was well over two minutes. She finally took his papers from the officer, asked Gary to take a seat and dismissed the officer.

While waiting, he wrote a letter to his mother explaining the situation and assuring her that he was okay, and also one to his Dad at his last known address in hope, notifying him that he was in the country and that he was being drafted into the army for the six months national service.

He sealed both letters, and approached the receptionist inquiring about a post office location. She took the letters from him, affixed a stamp to each, assured him that they would be posted, compliments of the KPR. Gary thanked her. She offered him coffee and a couple of biscuits, which he appreciatively accepted.

Waiting, he wondered whether the receptionist had any children, if a son, was he enlisted? He felt like asking her, but decided against it.

His instructions arrived within the hour; due to the high volume arrival of the British troops that morning, for the next two to three days the train would only be moving army personnel. He was ordered to stay in Mombasa and told that arrangements would be made for his accommodation during that time until further orders. It was approaching five in the afternoon, he was tired and hunger had started to set in causing occasional rumbles in his stomach.

About half an hour later, a serious looking young lady dressed in a khaki uniform entered the reception area, and asked about the whereabouts of the staff.

"They have already gone home," the receptionist said.

"I didn't realise it was that late," the other woman replied. She glanced towards Gary, with an enquiring look, as if to ask who the hell he was and what is he doing here? The receptionist said that the file had been placed on her desk over an hour ago.

She left and returned soon after and summoned Gary to follow her up a stairwell into an office on the second floor. She introduced herself as Inspector Karen Willis from Internal Security and apologised for having overlooked his file, also stating that the department that managed the conscript section had been moved to the capital city of Nairobi, and as the rest of her staff had already left for the day she would personally assist him in finding suitable accommodation for the few days needed.

"Do you have any relatives or friends that you would prefer to stay with?" she asked.

"No," Gary replied.

She excused herself to make a phone call and he heard her mentioning accommodation for one of her officers which somehow puzzled him, as she was supposed to be making a booking for him. He wanted to bring it to her attention but her "do not question me" look made him hold back.

She placed the phone back in its cradle, and told him that she had made a booking for him at the Palace Hotel, situated in the main street of the town and as she was about to leave, she would drive him over.

On arrival she escorted him to the hotel reception and they were greeted by the hotel manager. She took him aside and spoke to him in a low tone. Gary tried to listen to the conversation but with other noises around, could not hear what was said. The manager did glance towards him on a couple of occasions then walked over and introduced himself and as his was a rather long name, he asked Gary to call him Gerry.

"I have allocated you a room on the second level. If you do not find it suitable, or should you need any extra assistance, please do not hesitate to personally bring it to my attention," Gerry said. He then summoned a porter to take Gary's travel case to his room.

Without further comment, the Inspector turned and started to walk out, but suddenly stopped and told Gary that she would get someone to visit him on the following day with further instructions. Gary hoped it wouldn't be her, as he thought her quite officious and full of self-importance in that uniform.

On the way to his room, as he went past the reception area, Gerry informed him that dinner would be served in the dining room between 7.00 pm and 9.00 pm, but room service was also available should he prefer it.

Gary went up the stairs to his room, showered, and as it was a very humid evening, dressed in a pair of casual slacks, a short sleeved shirt and then made his way down the stairs to the dining room.

At the door he was greeted by the head waiter who escorted him to a table overlooking the hotel beer garden that was being well patronised by thirsty locals and their families, attended by well attired African waiters in white long dress uniforms as per the Swahili tradition known as *Kanzu*.

Without a solid meal since breakfast, Gary felt famished; the mixed grill from the menu was the kind of meal that could satisfy his hunger. Although the huge plate looked terribly overfilled when the waiter presented it, he managed to put quite a dent in his meal, apart from the lamb's fry that proved to be well down on his list of favourites. For dessert he ordered apple pie and ice cream, and devoured it all, finally washed down with a large glass of lemon squash.

After dinner he took a quick stroll down the main street, passing bars thumping out loud African music. The doorways of most of the bars were packed with drunken patrons, mainly sailors and soldiers leaning against one another preventing them from crumbling to the ground, while trying to attract the attention of taxis or any other mode of transport available, by yelling and whistling.

Every street corner, lamp posts were occupied by African girls of the night, offering their specialties to the drunken sailors and soldiers. The smell of spicy food on this still and humid evening engulfed the entire town.

After about half an hour stroll around the town, and having received countless offers of the services from the lamp post girls, he returned to his room, freshened up, leaped into bed and reflected on the day's events and although tired, sleep evaded him for several hours.

Chapter 4

He was awoken the next morning by a knock on the door from the room service waiter yelling *"Chai bwana, chai bwana,"* meaning *"Cup of Tea, Mister"* in Swahili. On the tray was also the daily newspaper. He took his cup of tea and newspaper, sat on the balcony overlooking the main street that looked totally deserted compared to the previous evening, slowly sipped his tea while catching up with the latest news and watching the few passers-by on their way to work, a favourite pastime of his. An hour later he showered, shaved, and dressed in the same pair of slacks he had worn the night before, a fresh, collared tee-shirt, left his room and went down to the breakfast lounge.

As he entered the lobby he spotted Gerry talking to a slim young lady with long auburn hair dressed in a pair of jeans and a white blouse who had her back to him. He was about to take a seat at an empty table when Gerry gestured for him to come over to their table. He could not believe his eyes as she turned around to greet him, that the young woman was Inspector Willis.

In uniform she looked like a woman in her late twenties, with strong feature and a no nonsense look. But today, this was just a sweet, young-looking, beautiful girl. Gary felt tense, he tried hard to utter a word but no sound came out of his mouth, and at the same time he could not stop admiring her. She greeted him with a warm smile and in a soft voice, said, "I hope you don't mind, I came to see if you were okay, and Gerry has kindly invited me to stay and have breakfast with you."

He was lost for words but managed a smile, indicating he gladly accepted the offer.

At breakfast they covered a wide range of topics. She was very interested in Gary's background and wanted to know more about the Seychelles, having obviously obtained all that information from his immigration file which she would have had on hand, as she seemed well informed about his mission of finding his father. She seemed a very friendly and intelligent person, she did not divulge a lot about herself and he did not press on with the subject either. They spent well over an hour chatting over breakfast.

She told him that she did not work weekends, and had no other commitments, so she would be happy to show him the sites of Mombasa and its surrounds, if he felt up to it, which he gladly accepted and thanked her.

Chapter 5

Born in Sussex England, Karen moved to Kenya in the early part of 1946. Her father a qualified accountant had taken a job with the British Government as auditor general, and posted to the capital city of Nairobi. She deferred her law degree that she was taking at Cambridge University for a year to accompany her parents. After several months in Africa she fell in love with the place, its people and the temperate climate, decided to stay and continued her studies via correspondence.

Being a bright student with credits and distinctions in her first year of University helped her secure a position with the Department of Internal Affairs. She worked and studied extremely hard, passed all her exams and later was moved to the Internal Security Department. She became a sergeant by the age of twenty-four and eventually an inspector at twenty-six.

However, when her father took ill a couple of years after arriving in Nairobi and died a year later from suspected chronic Malaria, she accepted a transfer to the coastal town of Mombasa as head of her department. Accompanied by her mother, they purchased a three bedroom home on the water front facing the harbour entrance.

Although not the best looking girl, freckled face, skinny, and a bit of a tomboy in her teen years, she grew up to be a beautiful young woman with plentiful admirers, had a few affairs with men slightly older than her, but never allowed herself to become too seriously involved with anyone. She had her mother often worried about her attitudes towards men, but she soon realised that she gave her career priority over men.

Being an only child, at a young age she was always included in all the discussions that took place between her parents and was encouraged to offer her opinion. She was far more advanced than most of her friends of similar ages and could converse with ease with the more mature persons. Her tomboy appearance that failed to attract boys in her early teens had made a complete turnaround and she was now the one that was keeping them at bay.

After her first year on the job, she had read and studied all the operational manuals, knew all the legal aspects and requirements of the operation, so much so that senior members were depending on her knowledge for their decisions.

She was smart, slim, tall, beautiful, with long auburn hair, deep hazel eyes, and high cheek bones, the type of girl one would only see in beauty magazines. She loved Mombasa for its warm, all year round climate and its great beaches, she was very popular and well respected by her friends and co-workers and displayed an all-over tan that would make most sun worshippers envious.

Chapter 6

They left the Hotel and drove east to the Old Town and once the main Port called Fort Jesus. She gave him the history as far back as the sixteenth century, when the Portuguese built Fort Jesus to secure their position on the coast of East Africa, she pointed to the site that was chosen, the Coral Ridge at the entrance of the harbour, close to the old Swahili and Arab town.

A tour guide would not have possessed better knowledge, Gary thought.

She told him the place was designed by an Italian architect and engineer by the name of Joao Batista Cairato, the then leading architect of the Portuguese in India. The plan consisted of a central court with bastions at the four corners and a rectangular projection facing the sea. The place covered an area of about two acres. When the British eventually took over, and the port was moved to the other side of the Island, Fort Jesus was turned into a prison.

They strolled along the narrow cobble paved streets that were used around the sixteen hundreds, when the Arab Traders following the trade winds around the Indian

Ocean, taking them several months, would arrive in their Dhows loaded with spices, bolts of fabrics, gold, silver and anything else they could trade. Most of those houses were still being occupied by local Arab and Swahili families.

From there they visited sites around the sea front, drove North East over the Nyali Bridge and on to the mainland, stopped for lunch at the internationally known Nyali Beach Hotel. Karen was a well-known person in Mombasa, She was fondly greeted wherever she went, and Gary got introduced to countless number of people.

Mombasa was a vibrant destination. Tourists from all parts of the world came here to visit the National Parks, or hunting safaris, including the serious hunters who came to bag the Big Five, killing an elephant, rhino, lion, leopard and buffalo and often taking trophies of their kill.

Kilindini Road is the main thoroughfare leading from the harbour, across the town and on to Fort Jesus, which was once the main port and town and is now a museum.

Loads of tourists filled the place, dressed in khaki safari suits, sweat marks around their chest and arm pits, giving the appearance that their suits were constructed from different shades of materials. They were loaded with cameras of every brand and size, leisurely taking photos of people, birds, shadows, cars, rickshaws, buildings anything that took their fancy. Investors in Kodak and other camera manufacturers would have been delighted to witness this.

This was Africa, the unknown, the mysterious land, where lions, elephants, leopards and all other wild beasts roam freely. Big game hunters paraded in their four wheel drive vehicles, displaying their built-in gun racks holding shiny guns of all calibres, obviously the shinier the armoury the more professional they would appear.

Safari tour operators drove around in their vehicles painted in striped or spotted design, representing zebras, giraffes and cheetahs, advertising their specialties and enticing customers to join their next great expedition.

Shops and restaurants around the town were bustling with hoards of American, English and French tourists who had recently arrived aboard the Castle Line ship and were out in force buying souvenirs from African and Arab peddlers. The bustling and hustling amongst the vendors trying to attract buyers were sometimes deafening.

Two Naval ships that were patrolling the Indian Ocean had also docked for supplies and navy personnel were enjoying their leave passes, frequenting bars and restaurants that were opened twenty four seven, the sailors getting themselves totally drunk by late morning. Military Police driving around in army jeeps and soft top Land Rovers were busily picking up the drunks and trouble makers and escorting them back to their ships.

Later on that afternoon they took the causeway that led on the western side of the island and onto the mainland where the oil refinery and airport are situated. People on that side of the town seemed to be living in an entirely different world, they moved at a much slower pace than in Mombasa less than a mile away. They seemed to spend most of their days sitting around and waiting for something to happen and by the look on their faces, they must have been waiting for a long time.

Karen eventually felt comfortable enough to reveal the reasons for her parents leaving England and migrating to Africa.

"My father was an accountant for the department of taxation in London," she said. "He worked there for twelve years. On several occasions he was promised a promotion as head of the audit department, and for three years running every time the position became vacant, it got filled through a political appointment, and he was made to wait again, until finally after being offered a job by a private firm, handed in his resignation. Instead of letting him go, they offered him this high profile job as auditor general of the whole of East Africa, based in Nairobi. They were confident that he would refuse the offer, but after talking it over with us, decided that it would be a good change and chance to see Africa and accepted the position.

"He did an excellent job, and was often commended for his work but somehow it also caused his death. The fact is that he is buried here and my mother refused to return to England. As for me I have Africa as my home and I will stay as long as it lets me."

With a planned dinner date arranged at her favourite Indian restaurant that evening, she invited Gary to join her. He was hesitant at first, stating that he did not want to intrude, but as she strongly insisted, he accepted. She dropped him at his hotel around five that afternoon and arranged to pick him up at eight.

Back in his room Gary laid on his bed and reviewed the day's events. He found it hard to believe that they had covered so much ground in one day, the longest distance he had ever travelled by car. He dozed off and was woken right on dusk, startled by a man's voice chanting some kind of hymn that resonated over the town consisting of a single word that dragged on for a couple of minutes without taking a single breath, as if amplified and was constantly repeated, and the whole event lasting for close to half an hour.

He later discovered that it was the usual evening ritual, emitted from a mosque two streets away announcing prayer time at sunset. Quickly showering and dressing for dinner, he went to the front entrance and waited for Karen to appear.

At the restaurant, he was introduced to Karen's two closest girlfriends and their partners, all of English origin. Both girls were lovely but somehow he sensed that one of the guys was very different, although knowing how to handle such a person, he still found him to be irritating and lacking in personality. Karen was always on the defensive and at times very abrupt, and even showed resentment towards him.

Gary found it hard to understand why such a beautiful girl as Karen did not have a steady boyfriend and at the same time was glad that she didn't.

The food was cooked with a vast amount of hot chillies and other spices which made it a highly tasty meal; there were curries, rice, chapattis, samousas and other dishes that kept appearing right through the evening. Despite the constant complaints by that particular irritating person about every dish that appeared, he managed to devour all that was placed in front of him and the evening was much appreciated by all.

After dinner, thankfully the irritating one and his girlfriend had other plans and Karen invited Gary and her two other friends back to her place for coffee and a chance for Gary to meet her mother, and later maybe visit the Town's well known night spot, the Florida Night Club, right on the water's edge on the entrance to the Harbour that was within walking distance from her place.

They arrived at her house around nine thirty, and were warmly greeted by Karen's mother, Denise, a very refined lady with a very stylish English accent. They had coffee, listened to music and talked for hours. Karen's friend's boyfriend was a friendly person, a keen golfer who worked for his father in the construction business and had somehow managed to escape being drafted into the KPR.

Around 11.30pm, as her two friends were leaving, they offered to drive Gary back to his hotel. Karen however insisted that she had to personally drive him back as he was in her care; furthermore they had made arrangement to visit the night club as Gary had never ever been into one.

Soon after, Denise also excused herself stating that it was way past her bedtime, leaving them alone. They sat and talked for a while longer and by the time they realised it was past midnight they decided to give the night club a miss. Gary wanted to call a cab but Karen insisted on driving him back to his hotel.

It was after 1.30 am when they finally arrived at the Palace hotel; even then they sat in the car outside and talked for another fifteen or so minutes, and made arrangement to meet the following day, but made no specific time.

Chapter 7

Karen arrived at ten the following morning with his orders.

He would be put on a train at twenty hundred hours, for the city of Nairobi, 300 miles away. There he would be met on arrival and taken by car to the KPR training Camp called Sergeant Leaky Barracks at Lanet, another ninety-eight miles near the town of Nakuru.

"There is a place that is very special to me," she said. "Since you are leaving so soon, I must take you to see it today. It is my refuge, and I spend all my spare time there, and I am sure by your description of the Seychelles, this place will bring back memories."

"How far away is it?" Gary asked. "I don't want to miss my train."

"Funny," she replied. "I would not want you to miss it either." She laughed softly.

"In that case, I accept you invitation," he said.

She drove down to the Likoni ferry that goes across the entrance of the harbour, that Gary had passed on the day of his arrival into Mombasa and took the car across to the mainland on the southern side, down past a secluded resort called Shelley Beach on to a dirt track towards a beach house tucked away in a bay right on the beach front. The place was tropical, secluded and private, a white sandy beach as its front yard. Gary thought that it did actually have lots of similarity to the Seychelles, although it lacked the mountainous backdrop.

Dotted all over were coconut palms, and other tropical trees. The water looked so inviting, that he opted to have a swim, although not having brought a swimming trunk he asked Karen not to look as he undressed down to his underwear and jumped into the surf, causing gales of laughter as she watched him trying to catch a wave with one hand holding his underpants in place.

They sat and talked about their lives, their goals, and expectation. Karen promised to help wherever she could in locating his Dad. They spent the whole day like a couple of kids who had known each other all their lives laughing at silly things, and enjoying their new found friendship. They were totally relaxed and before they realised it was time to head back.

Later that evening, accompanied by Karen and an officer, Gary was taken to the train station. Gary was finding it hard to understand how, with the supposed shortage of man power, the KPR could dispatch an officer to escort him to the train station. He was not even an enlisted man yet, and could have easily made his own way there. But as it was their rules, it was not up to him to question them.

While waiting on the platform, he spotted Anthony his acquaintance from the ship, walking down with his family, accompanied by some high ranking Army personnel.

Spotting Gary, Anthony wondered over to apologise for his sudden earlier departure, gave him an address and phone number to contact him when in Nairobi and also should he need assistance searching for his Dad.

Gary started to question of who Anthony really was, and came to the conclusion that he must be a very important person. Reflecting back on their earlier conversation, he remembered Anthony mentioning about studying Swahili and was just about to divulge the new position he would be occupying, when he was suddenly called away.

The officer who escorted him to the train jokingly said, "Gee, man, you have friends in high places!"

He told Gary that these officers were from the Government Intelligence and Security Department, and presumed that Anthony must be the new Department Head they had been waiting on.

Karen was well aware of his identity, as they were introduced on the day of his arrival into Mombasa. Being a secret squirrel herself, she would not divulge any information.

Gary was given his train ticket and placed in the fourth carriage from the front with about a dozen other passengers. The first three carriages were occupied and guarded by the army. The trip would take about twelve hours the officer told him, wished him good luck and left. Karen stayed and kept him company until departure. She left him just a few moments before the departure whistle was blown by a guard.

As the train pulled away she felt this sudden sadness. She tried hard to brush it away by telling herself that Gary was just another person that her department had handled and now that he was gone, her job was done and all was back to normal. Somehow the peaceful disposition about that young man had touched her and kept lingering in her mind. She felt angry and questioned her reasoning for having been involved in the first instance, but at the same time felt good for having helped, and she had enjoyed the time she had spent with him.

At home her mother noticed the change. Karen was sombre, walking around the house like a lost soul. Her mother dismissed it thinking that she was tired as she'd had an unusually busy weekend and left it at that. But somehow, several days later her mood had not changed and her mother then came to the conclusion that Karen might have fallen in love with Gary, but discarded that too, as her daughter was not the type that would easily fall in love.

Gary however was happy to have met and became friends with Karen. But ahead of him, another chapter in his life was about to open, although he was never one to show emotion, deep inside he really felt lost.

Chapter 8

The train built up steam, gave a few blasts on its whistle as it pulled out of the station right on time, but thirty miles out, came to a sudden stop at a siding for some unknown reason and there it stayed for two hours. While waiting, several thoughts went through Gary's mind. Being close to the main highway, he could hitch a ride back to Mombasa and there resume the search for his father. If the authorities lacked personnel to look for missing persons, they probably would not bother looking for him. Besides, he was not yet drafted. Then there was the issue of when the time came to return home; the KPR was holding his passport. He even contemplated changing his name and applying for another passport, which he presumed could be possible, but somehow his strict upbringing got the better of him and he decided against it. The shriek of the whistle and the sudden shudder brought him back to reality as the landscape started sliding by again.

The Indian head waiter walked down through the carriages sounding his Xylophone, announcing that dinner was served in the dining car. He checked Gary's ticket and allocated him a table that was set for one person in the corner of the diner. He was about to place his order when he received a tap on the shoulder. It was Anthony inviting him to join their table, where he was introduced to Anthony's wife Jessica, young daughter Corrine, and an Army captain with whom he was conversing. Both Jessica and her nine year old daughter were as pleasant and as well-spoken as Anthony. The Captain introduced himself but showed no interest in engaging in any conversation with him. Gary got on famously with the two ladies, they exchanged stories, and talked about India, the Seychelles, and other topics, while Anthony was engaged in discussion with the Captain who did not seem to have much to talk about outside military issues. At the end of the meal Gary thanked them for their company, shook hands with Anthony and the Captain and returned to his carriage.

He was moved to a sleeper car where the conductor made his bunk bed, and assured him that he would be woken up at least half an hour before reaching his destination.

He sat on his bunk and reflected on the day's events, thought about his mother, sisters, and little brother whom he adored back home, the chances of locating his Dad, the six months he would have to spend in the service, all seemed so hard. He realised that against his mother's will, he insisted and had persuaded her to let him go on this mission, therefore against all odds he must see to the end.

He laid down on his bunk bed feeling overwhelmed, when suddenly as if a flash of light had just hit him, he straightened up and realised the benefit of his acquaintance with Anthony, remembering their final words, ("give *me a call should you need assistance searching for your Dad.")* Tiredness and the constant rocking finally sent him into a deep sleep.

During the night the train made several stops, picking and letting off passengers, filling up their water tanks collecting more coal and mail bag drops.

He was woken early the next morning by another repetition of *"Chai Bwana Chai."* Opening the window shutter, he felt the change in the temperature that had dropped dramatically. Since leaving the coast, they had climbed to an altitude of over three thousand feet. Outside was a clear blue sky and the most perfect scenery he had ever seen.

The vast, open, flat land stretched for as far as the eyes could see, wild animals roaming freely, the consistent blasting of the whistle by the train driver warning them to keep off the track. They encountered wildebeests in their thousands, cheetahs playing games by attempting to match their speed against the train, herds of elephants, zebras, giraffes, and antelope dotted all over, foraging for any green shoots that may have appeared overnight amongst the dry brown plains that were badly in need of rain.

Gary was finding it hard to understand why although no fences existed along the railway line, the concentration of animals was mainly on the northern side. Eventually he decided to find someone who could explain and he finally found one of the train security guards who happened to be passing and posed the question.

"You are very observant," the guard said in a strong Indian accent. "A lot of people ask this same question, you will find it quite logical when I tell you."

Gary was expecting some way out explanation but the answer was quite simple.

"The northern side is part of the National Park, where shooting is prohibited," said the guard. "The animals had quickly learnt that they are protected on that side, and not many attempt to go across the railway line."

Nature is amazing, Garry thought.

At a semi dried lake, flamingos had gathered knee deep in their thousands along the shore. Their reflexions had turned the lake into dusty pink as the morning sun slowly made its majestic appearance over the horizon, its rays creating a shadow as it rose over the flat top Acacia trees and onto the savannah grass plain, flocks of tiny birds flying in unison, continuously swooping on insects being disturbed by wilder beasts making their migration south.

Gary knew he could never forget this astonishing scene.

Chapter 9

After being on the train for well over twelve hours, he finally reached Nairobi. He was met at the exit gate by an officer and taken to an Army base. After a short break and being given breakfast, he was introduced to his training officer who happened to be in Nairobi for the day and would be driving back to the barracks at Lanet that afternoon, and would escort Gary back with him.

Born in Rhodesia from Dutch and Anglo parents, Sergeant Thom had the appearance of an angry looking red faced man with gingery hair and a multi coloured moustache that looked totally out of place on his ruddy face. He had attended school in Johannesburg and moved to Kenya early in the 1940s where he joined the Kenya Police. He turned out to be an excellent communicator, and was sent to do a course in human resources and training in Rhodesia. On his return during the Kikuyu unrest, he was transferred to the Kenya Regiment as an assistant training officer and within a year had taken over the role of senior training officer and promoted to Staff Sergeant. He was well respected by his trainees and officers alike.

Along the way the sergeant gave him a quick history of Nairobi, dating back to 1896 when the Mombasa to Uganda railway was being constructed.

Needing a half-way point with flat ground, and plenty of water for a base to be established, after a thorough search between the two states, the only place that met the criteria was on the edge of the Maasai land that bordered with the Kikuyu land, named by the Maasai tribe as *Enkare Nyorobi*, meaning *Place of cool waters*. The base was established and the name was slightly altered to *Nairobi*.

With good agricultural land, cool climate and plenty of water, it soon started to attract Europeans seeking prime farming land and cooler climate and so the town developed around the railway base and kept growing at a rapid rate eventually becoming the capital city. The Kikuyu tribe lost all of their prime land when the white settlers moved in and expanded their claims further out, eventually to the point of forcing them off their land, ultimately to where the high lands of the rift valley became known as the *White Highlands*.

The prime Masaai land taken was only a small portion around the capital, therefore did not affect them a great deal as they were mainly nomads that grazed their cattle on the savannah plains, and unlike the Kikuyu did not cultivate their lands and grow crops.

Having lost all their prime land, the Kikuyu tribe was forced to vacate or work for the white settlers. Those who refused to leave their homes were classed as unlawful squatters. Finally the Kikuyu tribe started fighting back, they formed the *Kenya Land Freedom Army*, and this is what they were fighting today, Sergeant Thom told Gary with a slight quaver in his voice.

Gary recognised the sympathy that the Sergeant had for those people, but kept his silence.

The Sergeant went on to explain that the KPR was first formed in 1937 and remained at a low key until 1950 when it became active with the rise of the Mau Mau. He paused for a moment, and then said.

"The name 'Mau Mau,' no one knows where it originated from, and what it really means. All white eighteen year old males in Kenya are automatically conscripted into the KPR, the first recruit was sent to Salisbury in Rhodesia for their basic training, and from then on, all training has been undertaken at Sergeant Leaky Barracks at Lanet.

"The white people are given higher status over the Indians and blacks, in other words you will become an officer in charge of your patrol. Hence your special attention to date," he said with a wry smile.

"When it first started, few blacks were allocated rifles, those that were would only be given inferior weapons, but now we are giving them training, and issuing the more trusted ones with good weapons."

Despite his appearance, Gary found him to be an excellent and easy person to talk to, passionate about the Kikuyu cause, but against their method of retaliation, by the killing and burning of innocent people. He explained the dangers of home guard duties in which Gary would be trained, what was expected of them and in return, the duty expected from the people they were protecting.

"You treat your men with respect, and they will respect you in return," he said, staring at Gary, making certain that he was getting his point across.

The sergeant asked about Gary's background and his

reasons for being in Africa. Gary told the Sergeant about his parents, the school he attended, of never having seen or used a rifle before, apart from an air gun that his mate's father possessed, he told him about his growing up in the Seychelles, a subject that captured the Sergeant's attention, and he asked for more information, especially about the fishing and the girls.

The Sergeant was very sympathetic towards Gary and assured him that he would get adequate training and also wished him every success in locating his father when he finished his national service.

They drove up the Escarpment and stopped at one of the lookouts. Gary marvelled at the view of the valley in the distance below. From that height the animals grazing below looked like miniature toys.

From there they drove past Lake Naivasha on their left, stopped and admired the vast expanse of water and the native children playing along the water's edge while their mothers stood knee deep in the water busily chatting, washing their clothes and bathing in the cold water. A few metres away several men stood shoulder deep dragging their nets for fresh water crays, and further out in deeper water other men in their canoes were fishing for Naivasha Bass and Tilapias, while a few hundred metres away, herds of hippopotamus wallowed in the water unperturbed.

A few miles further, Sergeant Thom pulled up on the side of the road, and pointed to a monument erected a few hundred yards off the highway, displaying a sign that was too far away to be able to read. He told Gary that it was the exact spot where the Equator crosses Kenya. The countryside looked lush and amazingly beautiful, no matter from which angle you looked but the animals were not as abundant as on the coastal plains and Gary wondered whether the combination of the cold weather and high altitude could have been the cause.

Late that day they finally arrive at Sergeant Leaky Barracks at Lanet. Gary expected the place to be bustling, but instead found it to be quiet for its size, occupied mainly by senior Army officers, African police known as Askaries and the personnel that operated the barracks. However, late that evening exhausted patrols who had been on ambush, and home guard duties for well over a week, started arriving back, turning the camp into a more lively place. Apparently this was the day when patrols changed shifts. It looked like they had been in the same water soaked clothes for over a week, as Gary witnessed one of the men after having taken off his shoes, was having great difficulty removing his thick army socks, as they kept sticking to his foot and tearing off at every attempt and eventually plucked them off his feet in small bits.

He tried to converse with one of the patrol leaders, but the guy was definitely not in the mood for conversation.

Chapter 10

"This is going to be a crash course for you, as your duty will be Home Guard," said the officer in charge, talking to the men in the training room. They consisted of two English boys who had recently turned eighteen, two local boys from an Italian family and three Kenyan-born boys from Nairobi and Gary.

"You will each be given a good African enlisted man that we consider amongst the best we have, and three Askaries, who will stay under your command for the duration of your stay in the service. You will spend a week to ten days here, during that time we will give you all the training we consider necessary and we expect you to get to know your men. This is vital as they will become a part of your life for the next six months, and your safety will depend on them, as they are more attuned to the area than you are."

He went on to explain that home guard duty involved protecting families living on plantations or estates mostly out of town.

"These places are being attacked during the night," he said. "The attackers known as Mau Mau have a habit of intimidating the servants and forcing them to vacate the place. During the night when everyone is asleep, they barricade the doors from the outside preventing families from escaping while the house is being set alight, in an attempt to incinerate all inside.

"You and your patrol are to prevent this from happening. Your job is to protect the place and families you are assigned to. You must never ever be complacent and let your guards down, and never assume that things are okay, always make sure that they are, or it could cost you your life and those you are supposed to protect. Are we clear on that?" he asked.

"Yes sir," was the reply.

"How big are these gangs of Mau Mau?" Gary asked.

"We really don't know for sure," the officer replied. "We estimate them to be between eight to twenty or even thirty men."

"How would five of us be able to stop an army of thirty men?" Gary asked.

"You will be better trained and armed," Sergeant Thom cut in, "and your life depends on it." He grinned without humour.

"Thank you, Sergeant," the officer said before continuing. "Sergeant Thom will now take over. He will assign you to your quarters and will be in charge of all your training. He will issue you with all your Army requirements, including three months supplies of quinine tablets, with strict instruction to take one every day to avoid contracting malaria. He will then report directly to me when you are ready."

He stopped for a moment and stared directly and individually at all eight of them, then said, "A week from today, is that understood?"

He glanced around the room.

"Do you all understand that?" he repeated.

Everyone was silent,

"I can't hear you!" he shouted.

"Yes," Gary answered.

"Yes, who?" the officer asked

"Yes, SIR!" Sergeant Thom replied, and glared at them.

"Yes, SIR!" they all answered.

That night Gary found sleep hard to come by, firstly in a new camp bed and the soul searching of whether he did the right thing coming to Africa. He tossed around so frantically that in his sleep dislodged the mosquito netting that was anchored into the ceiling above the bed and brought it down over him.

"Maybe in the Seychelles mosquito nets are laid down flat," said Sergeant Thom as he entered the barrack for the roll call, "but here in Africa we find it to work best anchored to the ceiling. Would you kindly return it to its usual position?" With a smirk he walked out.

Training started with an early morning five mile run, followed after breakfast by shooting practice at the rifle range. By lunch time, they were a little more accurate on the targets, but all carrying sore shoulders from the mule-like kick delivered by the open-sighted Lee-Enfield 303 rifles. Sergeant Thom was however having a great day watching them go through the pain, and encouraging them to have a few more shots at the target.

Immediately after lunch, they were taken to the obstacle course track. Other then the Sergeant who was urging everyone to go a little faster that eventually turned it into a cross country endurance race that no one else found amusing undertaken on a full stomach. This was followed by other tasks that he found to be necessary that went well into late evening and by the time the dinner bugle call sounded in the mess hall, in staggered a bunch of sad and sorry new recruits.

More of the same happened the following day, followed by a couple of nights of patrol duty and a night of ambush, taking them through the leech infested bamboo belts where they lay motionless in damp areas supposedly watching a track used by Mau Mau sympathisers carting supplies. Although no one was caught in action, the night still turned out to be a very cold and uncomfortable one.

On the following morning the group was split up and each man was assigned to their own patrol. Gary's patrol consisted of four men, two of whom spoke a little English. That was just as well as his Swahili needed a lot more improvement. They were four tough looking men.

The head man was called Kelelu, a very serious, fit-looking guy, well-built and stood about five feet ten. He originated from the Luo tribe, and had made a carrier in the regiment. He was well respected and trusted by all his co-Askaries and officers alike.

The other was a man from the Wakamba tribe by the name of Rohan, who kept his head shaved and was also known to give it the occasional polish with bee's wax. It was so shiny that it gave a blinding reflection from the sun. He too had been in the force for over five years and was well trusted.

Next was Asmani a Swahili man from the coastal town of Malindi, He was a quiet and soft spoken man with a pleasant smile. He could not speak English but seemed to understand everything he was told. He was a solid looking guy and stood about five eight, and was in his second year in the force.

Last but not least was Joubert, a young man in his early twenties, who looked about sixteen, he came from the town of Tanga in the neighbouring state of Tanganyika, had a fair complexion and the appearance of a long distance runner. Joubert was previously a member of the Tanga police, and had recently joined the Kenya Regiment.

As requested, the group spent as much time as possible getting to know one another, they went to the rifle practice range together, kicked a soccer ball around the grounds. Gary listened and learned as much as possible about their individual backgrounds and their families and he also got the chance to practice his Swahili.

Chapter 11

Gary received his orders on the seventh day. His patrol was to relieve a unit that had been assigned to protect a couple of plantations neighbouring each other approximately sixty miles west of Nairobi. One was a coffee plantation and the other an orchard.

A long wheel base Land Rover was allocated to him with Asmani as his driver. Gary did not possess a driver's licence, but because he could drive, he was issued with an army permit that only allowed him to drive an army vehicle.

With their map on hand, they set out the following morning and within three hours arrived at their destination, covered in red dust. As the other patrol had already left, they were met and welcomed by the coffee plantation owner a man in his early forties by the name of David, and his wife Hilda. They had three children a girl and two boys.

David gave Gary a quick tour of the property. They had a workforce consisting of twenty-eight employees, a cook, a house boy, a Shamba boy, who looked after the house garden and twenty-five field workers, including the foreman, tractor drivers and labourers. Of the twenty-five workers, there were only four women in the work force and they were the pickers.

David was born in India to English parents. He had come to Africa in 1935. His father was an engineer with the British Railway and was transferred to East Africa to work on the railway upgrade through the Rift Valley.

Upon retirement, his father purchased this hundred-acre property at the base of Mount Kenya, constructed a Tudor style home, and started a coffee plantation. He first planted and cultivated ten acres then as his coffee became popular, added another ten acres. When David left school there was little prospect of work outside of railway or road work, so he decided to stay on the farm and help his Dad with the plantation that was proving to be a very lucrative business. They planted another ten acres. The house was extended when David married Hilda, eventually it grew into seven bedrooms and three bathroom home, with an extra two smaller homes and several workers huts scattered around the very leafy property, surrounded by tall fences and a large security entry gate.

He met Hilda, a French girl who was holidaying with her parents visiting East Africa at a dinner in town one evening. They enjoyed each other's company, and kept in contact. Eventually, while visiting his relatives in England he also planned a trip to France to visit Hilda who lived a short distance from the Paris city centre. He went over for the day and stayed a week. Later, she came to Kenya where they got married and settled.

The orchard next door was owned by an elderly couple from Mauritius who had four boys, but all of them had left home seeking work elsewhere. It was a small farm employing six people, again a house boy, Shamba Boy and a cook. It seemed that women were never employed to do domestic duties in Kenya.

The four Askaries were housed in a comfortable converted barn on David's coffee plantation and Gary was given a room in the main house.

After having had a long discussion with his men, and having organised the night's roster, he left them to get settled and rest. He went to the main house, made a call to his duty officer at the barracks and was advised to be extra cautious as there had been a couple of attempted attacks in his area the night before.

With good two-way radio and telephone communication systems between the two properties, Gary decided to leave three men to guard the bigger property and one on the smaller farm, where he would then make several visit during the night.

His Askaries, by their custom were usually fed before dark and were at their post soon after. Gary would then do his round and return to the main house around 8.30 pm for his dinner, and this suited him fine as he was never an early eater. He was also grateful to be getting his meals cooked.

The first night passed incident free, although news arrived the following day that several groups of Mau Mau were active in the area and an unoccupied house on a nearby property had been set alight. He was informed that for the next week, a couple of patrols would be setting ambushes in his area and would be in radio contact with him should they require assistance.

Ambushes were set in places where Intelligence had information of sympathisers taking supplies to the Mau

Mau camp during the night, usually by women and children. The ambush would be set to capture and destroy the supplies before reaching the camps, which were usually set in well-guarded, remote, dense bushes.

Apart from minor incidents, little happened for the next two weeks. The place started to feel like a resort, three meals a day, abundance of good food and coffee, nice clean comfortable bed, all in return for a night of incident-free patrols.

Eventually, their two weeks were up. They were relieved that morning and Gary thanked David and his wife for their hospitality and headed back to camp. They arrived at Sergeant Leaky barracks immaculately clean, well fed and having put an extra pound or two in weight. Gary was summoned to his senior officer's office for a complete report on the two weeks events. As he went past Sergeant Thom's office, he was called in and told to dramatize his report a little, which he did, and received his two days pass.

The next morning he took a bus to the nearby town of Nakuru where he booked a room at the Nakaru Hotel. After unpacking, he used the phone from his room to make a couple of calls regarding his father's disappearance, and one to Karen to inquire if she had received any further information. As she was out of the office, he left the number of the hotel he was staying at with her receptionist.

Within half an hour Karen had returned his call, and was happy to know that he was alright. She seemed eager to hear all about his first two weeks of combat, as she called it, although Gary could not understand what all the fuss was about. He found it more like he was on a holiday, but did not let on. She wanted to know if he had come across any danger and all about home guard duties. Gary promised to fully update her on their next meeting.

She then gave him the good news about his Dad. Apparently a couple of cheques which the bank verified as being his Dad's signature had been cashed within a period of four months, at two different venues near the town of Voi. She was waiting for further information to surface, although so far none was available. She also promised to come to Nairobi and visit him on his next two days leave pass, due in two weeks' time.

Chapter 12

His next assignment was a goat farm, west of the rift valley, 1200 meters above sea level. He and his patrol drove for the best part of six hours before reaching their destination. They went through some beautiful countryside and breath-taking scenery, encountered a pride of lions with four newly born cubs lying on the road enjoying the warmth of the morning sun. They were hesitant to move when the patrol approached, but after a short standoff they casually ambled off to the nearby bushes. They encountered flocks of wild guinea fowls, climbed for miles through deep fogs and eventually to a sunny plateau on the top of the ranges where the temperature plummeted, and sent them rummaging through their packs for warm jumpers. Asmani stopped and pointed at a branch of a massive fig tree. Gary tried hard to see what he was pointing at, but his eyes, not being attuned as Armani's failed to see the shadowy outline in the branches. Eventually he detected something swinging at the underside of the branch and to his amazement finally recognised the leopard well camouflaged among the branches. The movement of its tail was the only thing giving away its perfect concealment. Gary was relieved that he was not travelling alone, or on foot.

The farm produced and exported some of the best goat cheeses the world over, Gary was told by the owner, Hans. He was German, stood around six feet four inches, weighed over 120 kilos, all muscles, although Gary thought he sounded more like a South African but he assured Gary that he was of German descent.

The thousand acre undulating property employed seven white workers, four men and three women, all of European origin in their late twenties to early thirties, an Indian couple, and approximately forty African natives and their families. The European and the Indian residents were all within walking distant of the main homestead but the Africans had their own housing estate a couple of miles away.

The Askaries were again housed in a barn converted into comfortable accommodation, while Gary was housed in a small self-contained room attached to the homestead where Hans, his English wife Diana and two young daughters who happened to be home from boarding school during the holidays, resided.

Gary was given a tour of the property by Hans who turned out to possess a great sense of humour. He showed Gary all the vantage points of the property and also told him about an attempted attack approximately six months ago, but which was foiled when one of his Kikuyu workers gave him the warning.

Gary stood transfixed at the magnificence of the Rift Valley, mesmerised by the tranquillity as the sun went down over the horizon, passing through the flat top acacia trees, and the many peaks of the mountain ranges, constantly changing colours from deep red to yellowish, pink, blood red, and back to pink, something he had never witnessed before, and a moment he wished he could have shared with Karen.

That night he placed his Askaries at the key locations that Hans had pointed out, which gave them excellent views of the residence and its surrounds, while he constantly patrolled the area till dawn. The night passed without any incidents and so did the next two days.

At dinner on the fourth day, Hans told him that he would have to go to Nairobi to take care of some business, and at the same time, take the girls back to boarding school. He would possibly be away for a couple of days. Normally his wife would accompany him, but since the cheese production was at its peak, he would not be able to take her with him.

"I offered to get one of the girls to come and stay with her while I'm away," he told Gary, "but she refused, insisting that she will be all right by herself, so please keep an eye on her. As you can see Gary," he said, falling into a strong German accent after having consumed a few bottles of red wine, "*tose vomen are fery suborn, zey nefer do vat teh men says.*"

His wife having drunk a fair amount of red wine herself had the giggles. With blood shot eyes, looked over towards Gary and trying to imitate Hans's accent, she said, "*Vee Colonial Vomens are very tough,*" and kept giggling.

Hans called out to the house boy and asked him to prepare the sauna and invited Gary to join them. Not certain of what a sauna was, Gary declined, saying that he had to keep patrolling the area. Hans, being used to getting his own way insisted, telling him that he could go check on his men then join them later. Not wanting to offend his intoxicated host, Gary agreed.

Hans told Gary that he had personally constructed that sauna and wanted his opinion on it, although knowing that he could not give an opinion on something he was not familiar with, to avoid any embarrassment on his part, Gary agreed to drop in between his rounds.

An hour had passed before he arrived. Finding them still in the sauna, he went over and knocked on the door. Hans answered and told him grab a towel from the rack and come in.

He did as he was told, but was not sure why he should need a towel. Fully clothed, he entered and to his surprise found them and two of their European working girls totally naked and somehow laughing at him for having his clothes on. He went back to the change room took his clothes off, grabbed the towel and returned. Once inside he copied them by removing his towel and sat on the bench on the opposite side to them. The expression on Diana's face quickly changed when she saw his slightly bigger than average member and presumed that it was the reason for his hesitation in joining them earlier. Gary was feeling a little embarrassed as Diana kept giving it the occasional casual glance and the other two girls kept giggling. Hans, however was too drunk to take any notice.

After a while the heat in the sauna was proving difficult for Gary to breathe, so after about fifteen minutes he had to make an exit for a breath of fresh air and to cool down. He decided that enough was enough and got dressed again and returned to the house.

Again the night passed with little or nothing to report. Gary went to bed at dawn when everyone else was up and about, but failed to see Hans and the girls leave. He was not concerned, as he had said goodbye the night before, although he was not sure that Hans would have remembered in the state he was in.

He woke at noon, showered, and went down to the dining room where a pot of coffee was always brewing. The houseboy inquired if he would like some lunch, but he settled for the coffee instead and headed out to visit his Askaries who were already up. They discussed the night's events and wondered whether any changes should be made to their placements. As all agreed no change was necessary, he decided to leave the postings as they were and move the individuals around instead.

The factory was working long hours, the girls did not return till late that evening, he had dinner alone and returned to his patrol before Diana eventually returned home around 9.00pm looking totally exhausted, but glad that the task was completed.

The end of the week soon arrived, Hans had not returned but he eventually called his wife to say that he was held up and could be delayed for another couple of days. She assured him that all was okay and as the cheeses had been pressed and stored, there was no need for him to rush back.

Saturday night, a couple of their European girls and men employees came over to the main house for a barbecue. Although invited, Gary declined as he did not want to be partying while his men were working. However, he did go over at 8.30pm to have his meal. Diana and the two girls were in great spirits, laughing and joking, the guys had already left and Gary quickly ate his dinner and returned to his duties.

It was extremely quiet at dawn the following morning. Apart from the household staff, Gary was the only one at breakfast and was later told that Diana and the girls had slept till noon. Later that afternoon he saw Diana timidly moping around the house drinking coffee and swallowing headache tablets.

It must have been a good party, Gary thought to himself.

Gary understood why Hans's workers was so loyal to him and would warn him of any danger of attacks. He was a wonderful employer, looked after his workers, they all had good homes, he supplied all their basic needs. Once a week he shot two or three antelopes and provided them with fresh meat, the dam was stocked with tilapia fish and was at their disposal, he had a nurse visiting the camp and checking on his workers health monthly. A school was set up at the camp and a teacher was on his payroll, Water was pumped from the nearby dam into a huge holding tank on top of the hill and gravity fed to two places at the Camp, saving his workers the long walk to the river carrying buckets. They even had a wash house in the camp, although it was not often used as they preferred to wash in the river. On his return from business trips, he would always bring bags of lollies for the workers' children.

At dinner on Sunday, Diana apologised to Gary for having drunk a little too much the night before. He quickly shrugged it off by saying that they worked hard enough and deserved some relaxing time.

Later that evening they sat on the veranda for a little while and talked. She told him a little about herself, how hard they had to work in getting their business established, how successful their cheeses had become, about other avenues they could venture into and the fears that the Mau Mau rebellion had caused.

Gary was very sympathetic to their cause, but also felt compassion for the Kikuyu people for losing their land, although he did not dare to express his feelings.

Hans arrived back late Monday afternoon, and a truck loaded with supplies followed soon after. From his bedroom window, Gary watched it being unloaded, but failed to see any wines being delivered. At dinner that evening he posed the question.

"Where do you get you wine from?" he asked.

"We have our own vineyard and make our own wine," Diana replied.

Although Gary could not recollect seeing grapes being grown anywhere on the property, he figured a small vineyard must exist nearby.

"Come with me, and I will show you our cellar," she said. "Our grapes are grown on the hill next to the workers' camp."

She got up and Gary followed her down to an entrance under the house. She lit a kerosene lamp that was on a shelf at the entrance and there it was a well-stocked cellar. There must have been well over 3000 bottles of wine with hand written labels, dating back to well over ten years, carefully shelved.

"It's a shame that you don't drink," she said. "You could have tasted some of the best wine ever produced in Africa. Hans is an expert on wine making, his grandfather had a vineyard in the black forest in Germany and he spent most of his holidays helping him and learned all the tricks about making good wine. When Hans comes back I will get him to pick out a good bottle and you will have a taste. Yes?"

She sounded a bit like Hans when she said yes, Gary thought.

"Yes," he replied.

The next morning, new orders arrived for him and his patrol to stay for another week as heavy monsoon rain had washed away bridges in some areas, making it difficult to move patrols around. Gary and his men did not mind as they were being well looked after. They were assured that during monsoon season, the terrorist attacks were rare, but at the same time knew they could not become complacent.

Gary felt that he should call Karen and let her know and he got permission from Diana to use the phone.

He dialled the exchange and was instantly connected to Karen's office and spoke to her. He told her of the current situation and made arrangements to contact her as soon he had a definite date of his two days pass. Karen seemed happy to hear from him and said she was looking forward to their next meeting.

He thanked Diana and offered to pay for the call, but she refused to take any money, assuring him that he was welcome to use the phone at any time he needed to.

Another four days went by without incident before he received a call that his replacement would be arriving on the Friday. He called Karen to let her know. She told him that she would make bookings for both of them at the New Stanley Hotel in Nairobi for the two nights.

"It will of course be in separate rooms," she said, laughing.

"Why, not a double room?" he replied, trying to keep a serious tone. "We could sleep between the sheets, you know that you can trust me."

"I know I can trust you, but maybe I cannot trust myself," she said, laughing again.

Early Friday morning, straight from patrol the Land Rover was packed and ready to leave. He felt both sad and happy, sad for leaving this wonderful place and its people, happy to be seeing Karen, whose company he had missed so much.

Hans brought him a basket containing a bottle of red, a bottle of white and a large block of cheese. Both Diana and Hans hugged and thanked him, not only for his security, but also for his company, shook hands with all his Askaries, thanked them too and assured him that he was welcome to visit anytime he felt like getting away for a break, and to bring Karen as well.

They made it back to the Barracks within four hours. It must have been the downhill run, he thought to himself. After a quick debriefing, he took his leave pass, left a message on the notice board in the mess hall asking anyone going to Nairobi for a lift. After his shower he took his back pack and his gift basket, went back to the mess hall to see if anyone had responded to his message, but as there were none, he started making his way to the bus stop.

As he stepped out, an army captain driving a red, two seater MG car, called out to him.

"Where are you heading to, soldier?"

"Nairobi, sir," Gary replied.

"I can give you a lift, I'm going that way."

Within two hours, after making a couple of stops to where the captain called the watering hole(meaning pub), they arrived in Nairobi and to the captain's disappointment, Gary was a non-drinker and non-smoker.

"Do you have any vices, soldier?" he asked.

"Yes sir, I chase girls," Gary replied.

"Thank God for that," the captain replied with a grin. "I was starting to think that you were a fake."

He drove him right to the entrance of the New Stanley Hotel where Gary was booked for the two days.

Chapter 13

Entering the reception he was greeted by Karen who had arrived by train early that morning. She was wearing a pair of white jeans, silk blouse and a light pink cardigan. He felt so happy to see her and she looked so pretty. As she already had his room key, they went straight up to the fourth floor where his room was, right next to hers.

She told him about the reservation she had made for dinner that evening, but could be cancelled if he was not up to it, told him all about her train travel, while constantly bringing out little presents including a beautiful shirt that he chose to wear for dinner that evening. He looked at her admiringly as she continued talking for well over half an hour before Gary got a word in.

He handed her the gift basket. She opened it and exclaimed, "No way! How did you get that? Do you realise that no one can buy this wine, this is the best wine ever produced in this country?"

As she went through the basket, she also found the cheese and a note that Diana had written, that read, *"To the best security we have ever had, and the most easy going person heading it, we thank you Gary, we will miss you being around, you are welcome here anytime. Signed Hans and Diana.*

With slight teary eyes, Karen looked at him and whispered, "You touch so many people wherever you go. My mother and my friends think you are great, my receptionist having met you once never stops talking about you."

He quickly went over, took his hanky and wiped the tears off her cheeks, put his arms around her and whispered, "It's all right," then said something totally out of context to defuse the situation and make her laugh.

The weekend went well, they talked, laughed, Karen told him that she would love to be able to assist him searching for his Dad and she discussed the possibility of her obtaining leave when he was finally discharged from the service. Gary was a bit apprehensive at first, but agreed to discuss it further when the time arrived.

They hired a car and drove out to the restaurant where Karen had booked a table for them. The place was different from any other, the building was set on top of a hill overlooking the city. It was divided into seven different individual restaurants, decorated and managed by the nationality it represented and each restaurant accommodated around sixty people. There were the *"Grotto Capri," "The Tudor," "The Seine," "The Geisha," "The Riviera," "The Polynesian,"* and *"The Taj Mahal."* Each was totally separate from the other but somehow shared the same dance floor. Karen had booked the *"Grotto Capri"* that was designed like the original venue as shown in a photograph on the foyer wall. The meal was fantastic, they had some tasty Italian dishes, drank some imported

Italian wine from Tuscany, talked and danced till the early hours of Sunday morning.

After a late breakfast they took a drive around Nairobi, taking in the sites and its leafy surrounds then the nearby National Park and later met with some of Karen's friends for lunch. At 4.00 pm they parted company, as she headed to the airport for her flight back to Mombasa and he went to the bus stop to catch a ride back to camp.

As if prearranged, the red MG car appeared from nowhere, and a voice called out, "Where are you heading to soldier?"

"Back to camp, sir," Gary replied.

"That's where I'm heading," the captain said. "Hop in."

Gary got in the car and thanked him.

"Hope you don't mind the water hole stop," the captain said.

"No sir, it's part of the deal!"

They both laughed.

Dusk was setting in as they left the last water hole. Approximately twenty miles out past the Naivasha Road turn-off, they came to a bendy section of the highway that went through a mountain pass, around one of the tight bends that required a sharp reduction in speed. They heard gun shots, and found a couple of cars that had pulled up suddenly. Gary noticed lots of debris and tree branches scattered across the road.

"A tree must have fallen blocking the highway," he told the captain.

"That doesn't explain the gun shots," the officer said.

One of the vehicles was making an attempt to turn

around when gunfire broke out again. The captain told Gary to look behind his seat where he would find a handgun and a double barrel shot gun, and in the glove compartment some ammunition. Gary stretched across and retrieved both guns from behind the seat and prised open the glove compartment for the ammunition.

The captain pulled the car up close to the edge with plenty of bushes for protection. Gary grabbed the hand gun and handed the shotgun to the captain. As quietly as he could, he eased open the door and slid down the shallow embankment on the edge of the road. Once in a sheltered position, he gestured to the captain to do the same. They then fired a few rounds towards the attacker's position, at the same time motioning the occupants of the other cars to keep low and come over to their side of the road.

Once every one had arrived and were safely protected, he asked the captain to cover him as he made an attempt to run across the road.

With both cars headlight shining directly towards the attacker's location, he figured they would be blinded enough and possibly avoid detecting him running behind the cars to the opposite side. He asked the captain to fire a couple of shots to distract them as he made his way across.

The assailants retaliated with three consecutive shots towards the captain's position but as no shots were fired towards the cars, Gary figured that they did not see him run across to their side. He silently made his way around and ended up directly behind them. Through the glare of the headlights he spotted the three of them not more than thirty feet away, looking in disarray, each with a gun in one hand and the other hand attempting to cover their eyes. The car headlights were obviously affecting their vision.

Gary moved in closer until he was in a perfect position to take all three of them down with repetitive shots.

He remembered Sergeant Thom's words, *"You are better trained and equipped than they are."* He watched as they fired two more shots at the car's headlight, only one making contact. As they started to change the magazines on their rifles, Gary fired three consecutive shots low on their bodies in an attempt to only impair them. Two of his shots were dead on target, each hitting a man in his lower thigh, the third shot must have gone through their tin of explosives, which exploded into some kind of fireworks and lit up the entire area. Surprised, confused, and one of them badly burnt, all three dropped their weapons and surrendered.

He escorted them out of the bush and onto the road way, and with the help of the captain, was attempting to tie them up, when an armed patrol arrived, having been notified by a neighbouring farmer who heard gun shots.

The branches were cleared from the roadway, the patrol took the attackers away, and escorted the two cars and their occupants back to Nairobi. The captain and Gary continued on their journey back to camp.

The captain's report of the incident was somehow different to Gary's recollection. It read:

"The attackers were a group of approximately a dozen men who blocked the highway by cutting down a tree causing it to fall across the roadway, Two vehicles and their unarmed occupants were under attack when the off duty Captain accompanied by an off duty officer, came across the scene on their way back to camp. Always

armed while he travelled, the captain had in his possession a hand gun and a shot gun in case such a situation should arise. Through quick action by the captain and the young officer, under heavy gun fire they managed to guide those unarmed families out of their vehicles, and on to the safe side of the road, where the captain had them under his protection, while the young officer navigated his way across the highway to the attacker's side, and singlehandedly surrounded and apprehended them.

"He could have fatally wounded all three but chose to shoot them in the legs instead, and rendered them inactive.

"By capturing them alive, our intelligence is able to collect information that will assist in apprehending their leaders. The young officer was prepared to pursue the others, but the captain ordered him to abandon the chase for the safety of the civilian in their care..."

Gary shook his head in disbelief as he read the report. He was not asked to make one.

The news made headlines in all the papers and they both received a commendation for bravery. Gary became an overnight hero at the Barracks.

The next day's paper read:

"His heroism was brought about by the great training he had received from Staff Sergeant Thom and other officers at Sergeant Leaky Barrack. Early in the training, Gary's ability to

*take charge in a confronting situation was noted
by the Staff Sergeant.*

Gary was pleased that Sergeant Thom received a
mention but he found it hard to believe how facts could get
so distorted.

Chapter 14

"Your new posting is somehow very different," said Sergeant Thom, looking puzzled. "Resorts usually have their own security. Wait till I get more information from the duty officer, we do not have the resources for protecting party people"

He headed towards the Second Lieutenant's office and soon returned looking dejected and angry.

"I cannot get any straight answers from this mob, no one knows anything and no one asks questions. Typical army dominance," he said.

The resort was located approximately fifty miles west of Nairobi in a place called Hidden Valley, close to Lake Naivasha.

"I have never heard of a place called Hidden Valley," said the Sergeant. "It's not even listed on the map. I am aware of a resort in the vicinity, but I am sure it is not called Hidden Valley, unless the name has recently been altered. It's an exclusive members-only club, with their own private golf course, and is probably being patronised by judges, lawyers and high ranking government officials."

It took Gary and his patrol three hours to reach the place and then he had trouble entering the resort that was well guarded by their own security. After having been kept waiting at the front gate for over ten minutes, they finally obtained clearance and on entering were told to report to the head of security at reception.

"I'm Fred Parker. I did ask for experienced personnel," said the man who greeted Gary at the security office. He displayed a military-style short back and side hair-do and spoke in irritated tones while staring him up and down, as if to say, *you look terribly young, are you the best they have?* He told Gary to wait in the reception area while he returned to his office.

Gary heard loud exchanges of words in the office then a phone being dialled. After having waited for well over five minutes, Parker returned with a changed attitude and introduced himself, as the head of security. Feeling unfriendly after the hostile reception, Gary returned the up and down look, but said nothing.

Parker asked Gary to join him in his office for coffee. Instead of coffee, Gary asked for a cool drink and insisted that some be sent to his men waiting outside.

The security head apologised to Gary for his abruptness and explained that he had been under great pressure, having been given short notice on the arrival of some high government dignitaries from overseas spending the weekend at the resort. He hoped he and Gary would work closely together.

As they left for their quarters, Kelelu enquired about the confusion that seemed to have taken place. Gary replied that the man was either a smartass or was having a bad day.

Kelelu laughed and said, "Bwana Gazi, you are so different to anyone I have ever known. You are a young man yet you are so mature in your reasoning, and so calm in your decision making, no wonder we fully trust you."

The word *Gary* in Swahili means *Vehicle* although spelt *Gari*. His men, through respect did not want to name him Bwana Vehicle and instead changed it to *Bwana Gazi*. At first Gary thought that they had problem pronouncing the R but after Asmani had explained the reason, he did not seem to mind the name change.

From that day forward, he was known to his Askaries as "*Bwana Gazi.*"

His men were given accommodation in a bunk house near the entrance and he was given a room on the eastern side of the resort with views of the entry gate. It was agreed that resort security would cover during the day and he would take over during the night.

The high-ranking official conference held over the weekend passed without incident. Gary was woken at mid-morning on Monday with a phone call from the warrant officer, informing him that an extra patrol, consisting of five Askaries and a white officer had been dispatched to the resort and would come directly under his command. The warrant officer also advised him that the present private security company had been dismissed and he was to liaise directly with the General Manager of the resort, an ex-army captain by the name of Daryl Jones. Without further detailed information the call was terminated.

Gary had a long discussion with Daryl that afternoon. He thanked Gary for the weekend work, discussed the resort security and security needs for the week ahead, gave him a complete account of activities and type of clientele who frequented the resort.

"People like to drink and relax while at the resort and sometimes they also do stupid things," Daryl said. "Therefore what happens here we like keep it here." Daryl kept staring at him until Gary acknowledged that he had heard and understood.

Daryl offered Gary the use of the security office as his base, with phones and two way radios at his disposal, and on the wall was an aerial photograph of the whole estate, its buildings, roads, boundaries fences and elevation points, all of which Gary figured would be a great advantage to him and his men.

Since no reason was given for the removal of their security company, he did not find it his business to demand an explanation and the issue was not discussed further.

The resort was set on a twenty acre parcel of manicured, undulating prime land that overlooked the lake, a six foot fence with an extra two rows of barbed wiring running along the top protecting the whole twenty acres, first put there to stop wild animals entering the property, but mainly for protection against the destructive baboons and other monkeys that were in abundance in the area and caused havoc to the entire place, including their manicured flower gardens and the golf fairways and green.

The place looked magnificent with its carefully selected flat top acacia trees dotted around the place and some imported European Oaks and Maple trees displaying their beautiful foliage, roses of all colours covered the medium strip and both sides of the entrances. Dahlias and many other kinds of flowers had been carefully selected and planted in clumps all over the resort giving it an abundance of colours.

Authorised personnel and guests had entrance tags. Kelelu and one of the Askari were posted at the entrance, mainly for checking delivery trucks in and out. The place was well laid out; all guests' accommodations were built on small rises with views over the resort golf course and the lake.

The resort's main building and reception sat directly ahead from the main gate. Inside were two restaurants, theatre room, dance floor, heated swimming pool, sauna, spa, two conference rooms, gymnasium and two fully stocked bars. The road continued around on both sides of the building and on to the guests' accommodations and golf course.

The extra patrol arrived late that afternoon, led by an English officer named Malcolm Hall.

He greeted Gary. "I have heard so much about you and have been looking forward to working with you," he told him.

"I am glad to meet you too, Malcolm," Gary replied. "I'll give you a quick briefing of what we are doing here."

He filled him in on all the details, rules, and regulations they must abide by.

"I've asked Kelelu to organise accommodation for your men," Gary told him.

He then took him to meet Daryl the resort manager but as he was busy in his office sorting out the night menu with his head chef, he asked Gary to organise with reception to allocate Malcolm the room vacated by the previous security head person and arranged to have a meeting later that evening.

Malcolm found Gary to be less friendly than he was portrayed to be. But was envious of his class of leadership and the respect his men showed towards him, something he lacked.

At the meeting in Daryl's office late that day, he asked to be briefed on the security plan for the night. Gary detailed his plan of putting two men at the entrance, three on lookout from the three high vantage points, a couple constantly patrolling the fence line and two left off night duty to manage the gate during the day, but would be on call if needed. He and Malcolm would do checks and relief.

Daryl insisted that Gary remain in the security office from where he would monitor and control the operation and would be close by should an unforseen incident arise. Daryl's perseverance left Gary with no alternative but to agree and he assigned Malcolm to do the patrol and relief. Spending the night in an office was not something that Gary enjoyed. He contemplated sharing the monitoring duty with Malcolm, but the request was turned down by Daryl.

Dawn greeted them tired but incident free, Kelelu and one Askari settled at the gate house on their day shift while Gary and the rest of the night shift had breakfast before heading to bed.

Chapter 15

Early Friday morning, Gary was informed of the arrival of forty guests, booked in for the weekend. He was told that the Friday night party would be a fancy dress ball. As it was a private party, entry to their area would be strictly by invitation and it would be out of bounds to anyone else without a formal invitation.

"I know that you are not obliged to do that," said Daryl, "but you will do me a great favour if you would. I will need you to strictly supervise entry to this ball. You need to keep an open mind, these people are rich and powerful, if all goes well, you will be handsomely rewarded."

Friday evening, Gary had Malcolm and his men patrolling the main boundary away from the resort, two of his men at the gate and Kelelu at the front of the building in case he was needed.

The guests started arriving around 9.30pm, dressed as Geishas, Cleopatra, Mark Anthony, Arab Traders, Belly Dancers, Roy Rogers, and Billy the Kid. The party was well under way when suddenly Lady Godiva appeared, minus her horse but accompanied by the Earl of Mercia. Even though the venue was heated by two large fire places in opposite corners of the room, the temperature outside had dropped to a low ten degrees, causing Lady Godiva to cover herself with the Earl of Mercia's overcoat, to the great regret of the men present.

Four African waitresses and two African barmaids were in attendance, supervised by an attractive English lady in her late thirties or early forties. Music was being played from a record player and piped through four speakers standing in each corner of the room. Two waitresses stood in the foyer each holding a tray of Champagne for the guests on arrival, while inside, other waitresses were passing trays of *hors-d'oeuvre*. As each guest entered the venue they deposited their room keys in either one of the two baskets that was placed on a table at the entrance foyer, one had a blue ribbon tied around the handle, the other a pink. Gary observed that the men were using the blue ribboned basket and the ladies the pink.

They will surely have difficulty finding their keys at the end of the night, Gary thought, although from his prospectus it was obvious that the reason behind it was a lucky door prize to be drawn sometimes during the night. He somehow felt that a ticket system would have been more appropriate, but then came to the conclusion that people have their own ways of doing things.

The party kept up a spanking pace right through the night. Champagne was exchanged for wine, spirits and cocktails, the guests were consuming their drinks at the same fast rate as was being presented by the waitresses. As they became more intoxicated the party took on a more daring raunchy approach, some of the other ladies and men took turns on stage doing strip dances, a couple participating in an act managed to haul one of the young native waitress to the stage and attempted to undress her, while the crowd was clapping, cheering and shouting, "Get her gear off!" Gary figured that it must have been pre-arranged, as she did not show any sign of resentment, and later helped in undressing the man involved. The party became more audacious as the night progressed.

Finally in the early hours of the morning, the baskets were picked up and taken to the stage. Bored and tired, Gary contemplated what the prize could be. A set of golf clubs for the men, and gold or diamond necklace for the ladies, he thought. He didn't think a cash prize would be an appropriate gift. Somehow his boredom was replaced by an eagerness to know the answer.

One key was drawn from a blue basket and one from the pink basket, the winner from the blue basket, and the winner from the pink basket, held hands and they were serenaded out of the place, then the next draw and so on. It suddenly dawned on him what was actually happening. He could not believe that he was so naive.

He woke up at noon that day, went to the restaurant, had a coffee and a sandwich before heading to the office to plan the night's schedule. There he came across Daryl who was extremely happy with how the previous night's event had turned out. On his desk was an envelope and in it were notes totalling thirty two pounds in tips, equivalent to a month's wages to a well-paid person. Not certain that he could accept the money, he told Daryl that he would have to confer with his superior. Daryl's reply was that there were no rules in the army regulations which state that enlisted men were not allowed to accept gifts. Gary said that all the same, he would feel more at ease hearing it from his senior officer.

He was alarmed by a call that came from the barracks early Saturday, informing him that a patrol operating five miles from the resort, had intercepted a group of Mau Mau, shots were exchanged, one white officer was reported killed, an Askari badly injured, two terrorist killed, three captured and several were still being pursued. He was advised to be extra vigilant, as they had been informed by Intelligence that other groups, were also active in the same area. Gary also took the opportunity to ask about gift acceptance and was told that he could accept. Somehow, he did not specify that it was money.

The rest of the day passed quietly, with more guests arriving for the ball. Two Askaries were stationed at two high vantage points with views over the golf course where social games were being conducted.

From the office window he observed waiters, taking drink orders from players on the fifth tee and placing extra bottles in their golf bags that were being carried by caddies. Judging by the amount they were consuming, he wondered if they would ever finish the game.

He was interrupted by a woman's voice saying, "That's how the rich live."

She introduced herself as Dorothy the entertainment manager, who was here for the night's function.

Dorothy was a pretty blond girl in her late twenties. She told Gary that she had been in the hospitality industries for over eight years and had worked in several hotels and resorts around Europe. She had arrived in Kenya for a visit a year ago and was offered a job by a hotel management company in Nairobi to organise and manage international artists visiting Africa.

Saturday night's Masquerade Ball had been organised by her. She had hired a six piece band and booked a well-known international singer-comedian accompanied by a magic act. The resort had been completely booked out. Extra waiters, waitresses and a chef had been brought in from Nairobi to help with the catering.

They sat and talked for a while and she asked the reason for having armed personnel protecting the resort, which Gary explained. She was an interesting person, he thought, who unlike him had done a lot of travelling and he was eager to hear more about Europe and other countries.

As she would be spending a couple of days at the resort, they promised to catch up for a drink sometime during the evening after the party or the following day.

They came across one another several times during the night, the band ceased playing around 2.00am, but the party kept going till well after 3.00am.

Some of the guests had formed smaller groups, and retreated to their rooms, but the majority had called it quits. On his final round, Gary went past one of the rooms where some of the guests had gathered. He was propositioned by a couple of the girls to join them, but he politely declined the invitation, stating that he was on duty.

"How about you come here after work?" she said,

"You should be asleep by then," he replied as he walked away.

As he went past his room, he slipped in, had a shower and changed, a habit he had adopted since doing home guard duties. Then he headed back to the office and signed off his night patrol.

Back at the office, Dorothy was just finishing a discussion with some of her senior staff when Gary entered the security office. He had finished his paper work, and was about to leave when she appeared with a bottle of sparkling wine.

"Do we use your room or mine?" she asked.

He was taken a little bit off guard. "Mine is messy," he replied.

"Mine then, follow me," she said.

Back in her room she poured each of them a glass of wine, drank half of hers in one gulf, before excusing herself to freshen up. Gary heard the shower being turned on, settled down in an arm chair and grabbed the only magazine that was on the table and started browsing through it. She came out with only a towel wrapped around her, she topped up both glasses, dimmed the lights and came to sit on the arm rest of the lounge that he was sitting on and made small talk about a certain article in the magazine.

The slight fragrant perfume she was wearing wafted through the room with a pleasant sweet aroma. She started to gently caress and kiss his neck sending vibrations through his entire body and right down to his already bursting member that had not seen any action for over seven months.

Her towel had loosened and exposed both her lovely firm breasts that his wondering hands had found and were gently fondling. Her breathing had increased in tempo as he kissed the tips of her nipples that had hardened while moving his tongue gently around them, her towel had finally fallen down to the floor leaving her, entirely naked.

She slowly stood up, grabbed his hand and led him to the large inviting bed. She had taken the aggressor role and had him flat on his back, and slowly set out undressing him, kissing every new part of his body that became exposed in the process like an expert. She had his pants off with ease, she was more attentive when she reached the underpants, she slowly eased it down while kissing and massaging his throbbing Roger. Her mouth was working up and down the entire length of the shaft to the point where he could no longer hold back and he pulled her up to him.

While kissing her gently, he moved his hands down between her legs and felt the wetness. He tried to ease his way down to return the favour, but she held him back.

She had taken complete control, stayed on top of him and lowered her precious part on to his rock hard member and teased him more by pressing it flat towards his belly button and placing her wet clit on it moving up and down the shaft. To avoid coming, he shifted his mind to all the bad memories he had encountered during his short life. Eventually she paused for a moment and positioned herself to accepting him, she pressed the head of his penis into her wet opening and slowly accommodated the entire length, then withdrew it until only the head remained, again moved her body up and down only inserting a couple or so inches. She did that repeatedly by pushing eleven shallow stroke and one deep, repeated by ten shallow and two deep and so on while holding the deep ones for a few seconds and eventually to twelve deep strokes.

On reaching the ninth deep stroke he injected his load into her, and she responded with an orgasm that sent vibrations through her entire body. She later told him that she had read that method in a sex manual, and this was the first time she had attempted it. He somehow found it hard to believe as she was handling it like an expert.

Rays of the morning sun filtered through the room sheer curtains, as they laid there sleepy and exhausted. He asked her why she had not allowed him to return the oral favour.

She looked at him and said, "The only person allowed to do that is a girl."

He gave her a puzzled look, thinking it was a joke and wondering whether to laugh or not.

"I'm a lesbian," she said.

He gave her an intent look, as if asking for a more detail explanation and when none was forthcoming, he asked, "What is a lesbian?"

She looked at him adoringly. "You are so innocent," she said, and kissed him. "I'm in love with a woman, but I also like the occasional man."

Not understanding or trying to, he discarded it. They made love again but this time he took charge.

Gary walked out in a daze around midday wondering what had hit him. He thought he knew all there was to know about sex, but realised that he was a novice, and was very grateful for the lesson that had given him so much pleasure.

Back at the office that afternoon, Daryl informed him that a new security company had been hired for the resort and would like him to help them get acquainted with the place before his departure at the end of the week. He was introduced to their leader, a middle-aged South African ex-army man, who after leaving the service, spent time in the mercenary forces and was now running the security company. In the two days Gary spent in his company, never once did he see him smile. His dress style reminded him of someone he had seen in some early American black and white western movie. He wore a long sleeved check shirt, waist coat, leather gloves, and carried two hand guns on the belt around his waist.

Chapter 16

After having spent several months with his patrol, Gary had become fluent in Swahili and he could freely converse and even share their jokes.

Three months before his discharge, he was assigned to protect another family on a coffee plantation on the southern side of Mount Kenya where attacks were becoming more frequent. He was given an extra Askari, a Bantu Tribesmen by the name of Kumba. He stood around six and a half feet in height, and tipped the scale at around 120 kilos. Kelelu's description of Kumba was that if you talked to him for too long you ended up with a sore neck from looking up.

The place was owned and run by an elderly couple, Peter and Mary, both of English origin who had worked and retired in Kenya, and had owned their property for well over twenty years. They had been targeted on several occasions during the past year, once having a large portion of their crops destroyed, and the next year having their shed burnt down. Their loyal workers who refused to take the Mau Mau oath were murdered, while others deserted.

They had recently recruited new workers from the neighbouring state of Tanganyika.

The first two nights went by without a hitch, though news came of two neighbouring places being attacked, and although thankful, Gary was starting to think that it was all noise and no action. Little did he know that his turn could be soon.

A group of well-trained attackers had silently cut their way through the boundary fence, crept through rows of coffee trees and ended up undetected close to the homestead where Kelelu was stationed for the night, They were less than ten feet away when he spotted a few of them. Unable to raise the alarm by firing a warning shot, he took the only other option available, to directly open fire at the attackers. He fired three shots from his hand gun and wounded two. They returned fire with their homemade guns, filled with gravel and pellets, and shot him in the buttocks. Kumba was the first to reach Kelelu; they must have been deterred by his size and retreated into the bushes.

With the amount of movement through the bushes, Kelelu told Gary that he estimated they were outnumbered by at least three to one. He again remembered Sergeant Thom's words, *"You are better armed and trained than they are."*

He assessed the situation and tried to guess where the fence had been cut. Going by where Kelelu had been stationed, he figured it must have been on the eastern side.

He asked Kumba for his thoughts, he took his time looking at every angle, twitching his nose like a dog searching for a scent, then looked straight ahead, pointed to the north boundary and raised his open right hand three times, in a gesture indicating that there could be up to fifteen attackers in the group.

With Kelelu out of action, Gary was left with no other alternative but to trust Kumba. He asked Asmani and Rohan to move cautiously around the western side of the homestead and make their way north towards the inner fence that surrounded it, while he and Joubert would take the eastern fence, leaving wounded Kelelu and Kumba protecting the residence, under strict orders to only fire their weapons in the northern direction.

The plan Gary had put forward and adopted, was that once in position, they would repeatedly fire their rifles, firstly to pretend that more troops were present and also hoping the attackers would detect that all the fire power was being generated from three sides and none from the north, which hopefully was where their entry point was, so encouraging them to make their retreat in the same location, while he and Asmani, Rohan and Joubert would close in behind, and be in position to apprehend them.

The plan worked to perfection. The attackers hearing a barrage of guns being fired from all three sides must have thought that there were more troops than they had estimated. Panicked they attempted to retreat through their original entry hole on the northern fence and in so doing, ended up directly ahead of Gary and his men. They were falling over one another trying to get through the one man hole that had been cut through the fence, when Asmani yelled out in Kikuyu, to drop their guns and surrender.

They ignored the warning and Gary's troops opened fire, wounding six and capturing eight. Their leader who was still in the compound was yelling out to them to keep fighting. Gary went after him and just before reaching the fence line he turned around, with his long knife known as *Panga* drawn, he rushed towards Gary in an attempt to cut off his head, somehow missed and slashed him around the right shoulder and arm.

With the help of Asmani who fired a shot and got him in the foot, they finally managed to capture him.

At the house, the owners helped clean their wounds and slowed the bleeding from Gary's arm by applying a dressing tightly wrapped around it from elbow to the shoulder.

They tied the injured ones in the stone constructed shed, in a separate corner from those that had surrendered, to await transportation in the morning. Their leader who had been on the wanted list for several months, was handcuffed and tied to a post away from the others.

Dawn was breaking as Gary went looking for Kumba to thank him for his help, He found him sitting alone in a trance like state.

"What are you doing sitting all alone big fellow?" he asked.

"I am getting accustomed to the scent of the area," Kumba replied.

"What scent?" Gary asked with a chuckle.

"Scent, Bwana, is as important as seeing and hearing. If we use all three of those gifts that mother nature has given us equally, men would be more advanced than they are now."

Gary was intrigued.

"What can you smell right now?" Kumba asked.

Gary thought for a moment. "I can smell coffee," he said jokingly.

"Can you see coffee?" asked Kumba.

"No."

"What else can you smell?"

"Animals," Gary replied, wondering where this was leading to.

"Can you see the animals you can smell?"

"No," Gary replied.

"Now, Bwana, think about this. If you could train yourself to equally identify the things that your eyes and ears naturally do, how much better would it be, if you included your sense of smell?"

Gary just shook his head, uncertain what to say.

"I will give you another example," Kumba continued. "You hear a noise in the night, yet it is too dark for our eyes to see, your ears are able to hear, yet cannot tell what it is. If you could identify it by its scent, that would give you an advantage, would it not?"

Kumba was looking at Gary and waiting for an answer.

Gary stared directly ahead trying to digest it all.

"Every animal, plant, and even humans have a distinct smell," Kumba continued. "All you have to do is learn to identify them."

He walked to the corner of the shed, where the spice garden was, he picked six leaves, two each of mint, parsley and basil, brought the leaves to Gary and asked him to look, crush and individually smell them, which Gary did. He then asked him to close his eyes while he crushed each leaf separately and asked Gary to identify, and name each leaf from the smell. Gary correctly identified all three.

"There you are Bwana, you keep practising and you will soon be able to identify things before seeing or hearing."

It brought back memories of the old gentlemen that Gary had encountered on the ship, telling him about the distinct smell of Mombasa.

Their replacement arrived early in the morning, followed by the prison van that would transport the prisoners back to Nairobi holding centre and later sent to the Mau Mau Detention Centre in Mackinnon Road.

After being checked by a first aid nurse, both he and Kelelu were taken to hospital in Nairobi, while his patrol returned to camp.

Kelelu spent a couple of hours having pellets and gravel removed from his butt, while Gary was grateful for the cold nights of the Rift Valley forcing him to wear a thick jacket, which spared any nerves from being severed by the razor sharp pangas with which he was attacked and so helped minimised the injury in his left shoulder to only twenty one stitches and the chance of a quick recovery.

Late that afternoon, Sergeant Thom arrived to pick them up from hospital and take them back to camp. He looked a little concerned when he first entered the ward, but when he realised that Gary was not badly injured a big grin appeared on his face.

"The things you do to attract attention," the Sergeant told him then gently patted him on the shoulder and said, "Excellent work, Soldier."

Gary was given desk duty sharing Sergeant Thom's office for a couple of weeks. They got along extremely well. Sergeant Thom noticed that Gary was finding the desk duty extremely boring and was longing to be out and about.

With twenty-three new recruits that had recently arrived for training at the barracks, he was assigned to make random inspections on their quarters and on his second week was allowed to accompany the staff sergeant on a couple of training sessions.

Both he and the captain, who had become good friends were often invited by the sergeant and his wife quarters who resided at the base, for the occasional meal and a game of cards, which his wife also enjoyed.

Not wanting to alarm or worry Karen about his injuries, he kept communications between them to a minimum, as he normally did while on patrol. Karen must have sensed that something was wrong. She rang and left a message that she would be in Nakuru for the weekend. Wondering how she could have known that he was not away on duty, this surprised him until the captain presented him with a two day leave pass that he was not entitled to, and that made him realise who the culprit was.

After landing at Nairobi airport Karen hired a car and drove up to Nakuru, where she had two single rooms booked for the two days. Gary was grateful for the captain's generosity, as he totally enjoyed a weekend of being nursed and pampered.

Chapter 17

Back on full duty after the two weeks, he was to relieve Malcolm, the English officer he previously worked with at the resort who was doing a two weeks stint on a rather large peas and beans plantation on the Naivasha road.

He and his men arrived early that morning. Malcolm, having enjoyed an excellent relationship on their previous assignment at the resort, decided to wait for his arrival and familiarise him with the place. At the residence he was introduced to the owner, an elderly gentleman by the name of Jim, no mention was made of a wife being around. As Gary's men were settling in, Malcolm took him on a tour of the perimeter of the property that was guarded by high electrified fences, again to keep monkeys and other predators from damaging the crops.

He warned Gary that unlike other properties, the owners of this place were not as friendly. In fact they are a little hostile, even towards each another, he said.

"What do you mean by hostile?" Gary asked.

"Well," said Malcolm, "I've been here for two weeks, and he spoke to me twice and as for her, she won't even acknowledge that I am around, and the guy that I replaced told me the same thing. He is twice her age and have three children, and one of them looks black."

"He may be adopted," Gary said.

"Maybe, but trust me, they are from another planet."

Gary thanked him as he and his patrol left.

This time, his accommodation was in a spare building next to the main house. It had a kitchen, bathroom with separate toilet, a well-stocked fridge, and to his surprise, he was allocated his own house boy/cook.

After unpacking, he walked over to check on his men. He found them settled and enjoying a game of dominos. He returned to his dwelling and sat in one of the two chairs on the veranda, which happened to be a very old, comfortable rocking chair and was admiring the expansive acreage of lush green fields, cultivated in rows of peas and beans that spread across the entire clearing. Movement caught his attention on the eastern boundary a couple of hundred yards away. He stood up to get a proper view and to his amazement a troop of monkeys was attempting to climb over the fence, although constantly being zapped by the 2000 volts power delivered by the electric fencing which sent them flying in the air and landing back on the ground several feet away, stunned.

Gary could not resist bursting out with laughter, he was astounded by their persistence in repeatedly continuing to climb back up and touch the same high voltage wirings, as if enjoying the thrill.

The place employed thirty full time workers and during picking seasons, an extra seventy casual pickers were brought in.

Gary and his men were out on patrol by the time the wife arrived, he presumed that she could have been in town shopping. The three children were very young boys. From a distance he noticed that the eldest was barely six and the youngest maybe two years old. He could not detect any difference in colour from where he was. They were all addressing her as Mum.

The first night passed incident free. He went to bed as soon as it got light around 5.30 am the following morning and slept till around noon. He was walking towards his men's bunk house, when he was greeted by a lady who introduced herself as Jim's wife. She was in her mid to late twenties and at first he thought that it was his daughter but when she said wife, he remembered what Malcolm had said.

Although a little timid, she was a pleasant enough person, She was solidly built with short blond hair, the bloodshot eyes giving an indication that she was either a heavy drinker or was lacking sleep, and she was a smoker, judging from the smell of tobacco on her.

 He was approached by Jim later that afternoon and was invited to the house for drinks and to meet the family.

"Come around five," Jim said.

"I will," Gary assured him. Things didn't seem to be much like Malcolm had said.

He arrived on the dot of five as, their house boy was serving drinks on the veranda and Jim introduced him to his wife, Anita. Gary was about to say that they had met earlier, when she gave him a stern look, walked over and shook his hand, and said, "I am Anita, glad to make your acquaintance."

She was being very formal, he thought. The children were nowhere to be seen. Obviously they were being cared for by the servants. After partaking in a glass of wine and exchanging a few pleasantries, he excused himself, by saying he had to go check on his men and left. He did however detect a bit of tension between the wife and husband.

Little happened for the next two days. Jim and Anita ran a very quiet and simple household and they were both early sleepers and risers.

The weekend arrived and Jim left early Saturday morning. Gary was woken up by a knock on his door around noon. Anita apologised for disturbing his sleep and although he assured her that he was already awake, she still kept apologising.

"Jim has asked me to tell you that he may be away for a couple of days," she said. "He was going to let you know personally, but he missed seeing you before you went to bed, so he asked me to tell you of his absence. I will be going to visit my friend a few miles away and should be back before dark."

She sounded a little anxious while delivering the message, Gary thought, but apart from that, he found her pleasant enough.

Anita was back well before dark. Although he did not personally see her, he noticed that the car was back in the car port.

With his men at their post, he settled back in the old rocking chair that he had grown so fond of and was rocking back and forth when he received a call from Kelelu stationed approximately a hundred yards from the residence, telling him that he had noticed some unusual activities at the main house.

Gary slowly got himself from the chair and went to investigate. He noticed a dimly lit lamp in one of the unused upstairs bedrooms. He made the kitchen his first point of call and found it empty and so was the dining room. He became alarmed, as the house boy was normally in the kitchen cleaning up at that hour.

Knowing that Kelelu would have the place in his sight, he drew his gun and cautiously ascended the outer wooden stairs of the veranda that led towards the bedroom in question, holding his breath with every step he took and being careful to avoid putting extra pressure on the creaky boards. On reaching the door he heard movements and whimpers from within. He peered through the gap of the slightly open door, and to his horror, found Anita totally naked pinned under the house boy also naked, engaged in very active sex. The Samba boy was standing at the inner door at the darker corner of the room, watching the spectacle and fondling himself.

From the angle he was at, it looked very much like she was being raped.

He steadied himself, before kicking at the door and once inside he pointed his gun at the houseboy who looked totally surprised by his intrusion but didn't seem frightened. The Shamba boy had slipped out of the room through the inner door.

Gary realised that Anita had consented to having sex with the house boy and the Shamba boy had slipped in unnoticed, watching them. Gary felt embarrassed by his intrusion.

Not wanting to look stupid, he asked, "Are you all right?"

There was silence for a minute, before she dismissed the house boy by saying "*ondoca*," meaning "Go away" in Swahili. He quickly left.

She was drunk, naked and not making any attempt at covering herself. Gary apologised and left. He went back out to his unit to get a drink of water and try to gather himself up, when she suddenly entered and sat down in a chair opposite him.

"Please do not pass judgement on me until you hear my side of the story," she said nervously. "This whole thing is my husband's fault."

"I am sorry," Gary said. "I was only concerned about your safety. Knowing now that you're safe, I don't need any explanation."

"No, please, you must listen to me," she said.

Rather than cause any more embarrassment, Gary nodded.

"I come from a very disturbed childhood," she said, staring out towards the dark open field. "My father was a cruel and violent man who constantly abused my mother and elder brother. I ran away from home at an early age, and lived on the streets for several months. I got mixed up with the wrong crowds and ended up in trouble with the police.

"I was placed with a foster family in Nakuru who did not treat me any better. Jim happened to be their friend, that's how I met him. He was much older than me but he seemed kind and showed a lot of compassion towards me. I was eighteen and wanted an out, so when he asked me to marry him, all I could think of was the security he could provide for me and a place of my own so I did not let the age difference deter me.

"Our first few years were great, He was never a great lover, drank a lot, and always had pre-ejaculation problems or when he was too intoxicated he would spend all night trying. I remember our first encounter. He came all over me before he even got my panties off. The doctor kept telling him that his problem was due to heavy drinking but he could not give up. Eventually I started drinking too.

"We haven't been able to have sex for a couple of years now, he even has problems getting an erection and the few times we were able to only ended with him coming prematurely, and left me wanting to climb the wall."

Gary had not heard that expression before and was wandering what wall she intended to climb, when it suddenly dawned on him what she was talking about. It nearly made him laugh but he managed to keep his composure. She seemed to have suddenly sobered up, as she continued.

"One night we both had a lot to drink and attempted to have sex. We tried for hours but he failed to get an erection, He left me so frustrated that I threw a pot plant at him and cried for hours."

The whole thing was dragging on and Gary did not want to hear any more of the gory details. He was constantly looking at his two way radio wishing that one of his men would call, but since that did not happen he started looking for excuses, but found it hard to suddenly ignore her and walk away.

"I brought up the subject a few nights later, that maybe I should find a lover," she continued. "But he was against that, his argument being that a lot of marriages have been ruined by women having extra marital affairs and he did not want that to happen to us.

"Then one evening he told me that he had found a solution, saying that he had spoken to one of his friends in Nakuru who was having the same problem as he was, and suggested that we use our house boy to satisfied my need, and not jeopardise our marriage, because I would not want to run off with him, as he could not afford to support me. I told him that he was out of his mind if he thought that I would be sleeping with my house boy.

"I was never allowed to associate with any of the officers that came here to do home guard duties, this is why the other day when we were introduced, I pretended that I hadn't met you earlier, just to avoid an argument. He is a very jealous old man, he would kill both Doni and I if he found out what took place behind his back. Please don't tell him."

"I was only concerned with your safety," Gary said. "Since you're okay, all is forgotten. But what about the Shamba boy? Is he liable to say something?"

"What about the Shamba boy?"

"He was standing in the corner of the room watching you and Doni."

She looked shocked for a moment, and then gained her composure. "The dirty little rat! I will get Doni to talk to him." After a slight hesitation, she continued. "I was out shopping with my girlfriend who I confided in a few days later. I told her of what had transpired between Jim and me and to my surprise, she laughed and said, 'Darling every white woman I know here has sex with their house boy. Why do you think we only keep the good looking ones? We always pick the more handsome and well hung ones, as long as our husbands don't find out. To safeguard ourselves, we tell our house boy that if it ever gets out, we will say that they raped us. They know the consequences of what will happen to them if it ever gets out. But if you ever do it, which like the rest of us, you eventually will, let it be your secret, never divulge it to anyone.'

"It left me a bit stunned," Anita said. "It had never crossed my mind to sleep with my house boy or any black man. One night after having consumed a large amount of wine, Jim called Doni in, and asked him to give me a massage. I objected at first, but then found no harm in it. He had strong hands and seemed to know what he was doing. It felt good on my back and shoulders. Jim brought out some baby oil and told him to start by massaging my legs, we had some more wine and Jim poured Doni a glass as well.

"The oil was going all over my good dress, Jim asked me to take them off, which I did, but kept my bra and panties on. After another glass or two, Jim removed my bra and applied more oil on my then aching breast. Doni's clothes were getting oil soaked too, and Jim helped him out of his shirt. Although in his forties he had a nice and muscular body. After a while Jim asked him to remove his trousers, and just to keep his underpants on. He hesitated. Thinking that he may be shy, I turned my head away.

"Since that did not help either, Jim insisted that he did and eventually he started to undo his belt and as he unzipped his pants, out popped this massive stiff penis that had slipped out of his old stretched underpants, and he was fighting a losing battle trying to guide it back in. I felt so sorry for him. He was so worked up that the head of his penis had turned purple and although I could not stop looking at it, I had no intention of letting it near me.

"Jim must have got turned on by it all, he had his zip undone and his old fellow out at half mast. He told Doni to go wait outside while he pulled me down towards him to the bottom of the bed, parted my undies to the side and ejaculated as soon as he penetrated, leaving me covered with his sperm and again frustrated.

"My resistance to having sex with my house boy was gradually lessening. I asked for another drink. He called Doni back in, and asked him to bring another bottle of wine. His penis was no longer bursting out of his underpants, so I figured that he must have had a wank outside and I was the only one between us three left high and dry.

"He rubbed more oil around my lower body and kept massaging and every now and then his penis, that had started to come alive again would touch part of my body, either intentionally or not, as he moved around. I was starting to enjoy this tease when Jim got up and told him that it was enough, and asked him to go.

"A few nights later, the same thing happened, except this time I undressed to my undies before the massage started, and Jim repeated the previous version of watching the massage, having his way with me while Doni waited outside, and his quick ejaculation, again leaving me frustrated. However, this night he must have consumed a little too much alcohol so that after finishing his deed, he fell asleep on the lounge chair where he usually sat like a maestro directing the show, leaving Doni unsupervised. Doni did the usual oil rub on my back then like an expert ordered me to turn over, he massaged my breasts and down to my stomach and then moved his hands around my crutch.

"I did not offer any resistance when he pulled me down towards him, and in a flash had his penis that was lubricated in baby oil penetrating me, and slowly forced over half of it into me till he could fit no more as it had bottomed out, and caused me some pain as he held it there for a moment.

"My dignity and care had gone at that stage, all I wanted was to feel his manhood pushing into me, we got into this wild inhibited rhythm that was driving us both to ecstasy when Jim suddenly stirred in his chair. Scared, Doni attempted to pull out, but I held both my legs tightly around him, forcing him to inject his load deep inside me, his constant repeated thrusts brought me to a sudden massive orgasm like I never had before.

"Scared that Jim would wake up and find him around, he quickly gathered his clothes and left, leaving me lying there in a pool of messy sperm, totally satisfied and too exhausted to give a dam or bother to clean myself up.

"The next morning I woke up feeling ashamed and violated. I hated Jim for what had happened and Doni for taking advantage of me. I spent an hour in the shower trying to wash myself clean, hoping it would all go away.

"For the next two weeks, I refused to be any part of Jim's perverted act, but soon the desire to have sex with Doni returned, the yearning for having him inserting the entire length of it into me kept me awake for several nights. And our next encounter took place on the kitchen table in broad daylight one morning, while Jim was in the shower and the children were still sleeping.

"One thing I have discovered is that sex has nothing to do with love. I was led to believe that unless you love someone you could not enjoy sex, but I now know different it is for me a way of releasing tension within oneself. I fully understand why these ladies, like my friend on properties away from civilisation find satisfaction in their house boys. So nine months later I gave birth to a half dark baby, which I love dearly. I told Jim that my grandfather was a half-caste Pacific Islander, and the baby could be a throw-back.

"This is as true as I stand here today. I hope you respect my wish and keep it strictly a secret."

Her sobbing had intensified, tears were freely flowing down both her cheeks. Feeling bad about the intrusion, Gary put his arm around her to comfort her, and assured her that he wasn't one to judge others, and walked her back to her house.

At her entrance door, he gave her a peck on the forehead, and said, "Your secret is safe with me," then left.

Anita felt like a load had been lifted, she went in and took another long shower again in an attempt to wash away all bad omens that were controlling her life. Lying in bed she found it hard to comprehend what came over her to make her divulge all her secrets to a stranger, and to be touched by him to such an extent.

Back on his round, Gary reflected on it all and could not believe what had just happened. Bewildered he tried to put it to rest. But the story caused his mind to wonder back to the other places he had done guard duties and things that he had noticed and passed it as normal then, but now he started having doubts as he reflected on other housewives he had encountered. Did they all have some dark secrets? he wondered. Africa was really proving to be a learning place for him.

Chapter 18

After a few more home guard and ambush duties, his six months term was up. His discharge papers had arrived although he was kept in the Reserve and asked to report once a week for as long as he resided in Kenya. Otherwise, he was free to resume the search for his Dad.

Asmani had also taken his discharge and wanted to return home to his family in the coastal town of Malindi. He had timed his discharge to correspond with Gary's so that they could drive back to Mombasa together and he even offered to help in locating his Dad before he eventually returned home. Although very touched by his offer Gary did not wish to take advantage of his assistance as he was in no position to pay for his services, even though Asmani had assured him that he did not expect to be compensated.

With no desire to make irrational decision in accepting his help, he was happy to give him a lift to Mombasa.

Karen was extremely excited, to have him back. Her colleagues at work noticed the sudden change in her attitude, she was happy, more open and approachable and displayed a continuous smile. She had asked Gary to take the first train down and stay at her house while he organised the search for his father.

He remained in Nairobi for a couple more days and obtained his driver's licence which was easy, as having an army driving licence automatically made him eligible for an international drivers licence. He purchased a second-hand, long wheel base Land Rover, obtained some necessary items from the disposal store, including fuel cans, water containers, a set of wheel chains, and extra spare wheel, puncture repair kit, a two-men tent and an extra sleeping bag should Karen insist on coming with him, a kerosene cooker, a couple of pots and pans, a kettle, two mugs and a shovel. At the grocery store, he bought coffee, tea, cans of corned beef, baked beans, green peas and a few more items. At the gun shop he purchased a shot gun, a hand gun and a .22 magnum rifle, with a few extra boxes of ammunition.

He dug out Anthony's business card from his wallet, went to the pay phone and called his office number. A lady answered the phone.

"May I speak to Mr Phillips?" Gary asked.

"May I say who is calling?"

"My name is Gary, I met him on the ship," he told her.

"What is it about?" she asked.

"It is a personal call, will you kindly get him for me please," Gary said.

"How do you spell your name?" she asked.

Gary slowly spelt it out, she repeated the spelling and got a couple of letters wrong. He corrected her.

After a lengthy pause, Anthony answered.

"Gary! How are you and where are you?" he asked.

Gary told him that his six months service was up and would be leaving for Mombasa soon to resume the search for his Dad but wanted to touch base before he left.

"You must come and spend a few days with us before you leave," said Anthony. "Do you want me to send a car for you?"

"I have transport," Gary replied.

"Let me give you my address and come right over. I will be leaving my office shortly, looking forward to seeing you."

Gary wrote down the address, and hung up.

He arrived at Anthony's place within the hour. Being in an old Land Rover, dressed in civilian clothes without a security pass, all made it difficult to enter a high security Army Headquarters, something Anthony had forgotten to tell him, but luckily he arrived soon after and was able to clear him through the gates.

Both Anthony and his wife Jessica made Gary feel very welcome to their home, Jessica fussed over him like a mother who had just found her lost son and spoilt him for the whole two days that he spent there. She had all his clothes washed and pressed, they showed him the sights of Nairobi, introduced him to their friends and took him out to dinner. Gary felt totally at home and relaxed and on the day that he was leaving, Anthony made him promise to keep in close contact, gave him the name, and contact number of the head person in his Mombasa office, who turned out to be Karen.

"I believe you are already acquainted with the inspector," he said. "She still remembers you from the day of your arrival. She will see that you get all the assistance you will require."

Gary thanked him and Jessica for their hospitality and left.

On his way out of town he called and picked Asmani up, as previously arranged and agreed that he would be good company and also help with the driving.

The monsoon rain was into its third month and a really heavy downpour had already occurred in some areas. The bitumen road ended approximately ten miles out of Nairobi and from there they were on the slippery and wet dirt muddy road that sent the Land Rover into a slide. They pulled up, engaged into four wheel drive and greatly lowered their speed.

Along the way they came across several road signs indicating the road was only suitable for four wheel drive vehicles. Somehow, it did not deter the locals attempting the crossing in their Vauxhalls, Fords and Volkswagens and often their vehicle was found abandoned on the side of the road or half way in a creek.

Approximately twenty miles further, they came across a road closure where three trucks attempting to cross a low area, had bogged down to their axles. A grader that came to their rescue met with the same fate, leaving the highway completely blocked.

With no other way of getting around, and going back which could take hours was out of the question, they decided to stay and wait, along with the thirty-odd other vehicles that were already there, patiently waiting for a break in the weather.

The place must have resembled a used car lot or a market place, when some of the local natives arrived from nearby villages, with baskets of hard boiled eggs, selection of fruits, corn and tomatoes that they were selling.

By morning, rain had abated slightly, the arrival of another Grader to clear the highway brought hope to all patiently waiting but it too met with the same fate, blocking the highway even further.

The forecast received from the road maintenance workers indicated that rain would continue for at least another two days, and would possibly take a full day of sun after that to make it passable.

Asmani told Gary that he had knowledge of a camp occupied by the Kamba tribe about five miles back from where they were. He had worked there as an Askari doing peace keeping during the tribal unrest between the Maasai and Wakamba tribe a couple of years before and had made a few friends that he could call on. The road went through some black cotton soil that was extremely slippery, but since it was not commonly used by a lot of traffic, using their chains would enable them to get through. With no other option on hand Gary decided to give it a try.

An hour later they entered the camp that consisted of a dozen or so rounded huts, with thatched roofs, their sides roughly plastered with mud that was slowly being eroded by the heavy rain, leaving wide gaps showing daylight through the walls. The corn plantation was knee deep in water and apart from smoke coming from several huts, the place looked totally deserted. They pulled up on a high ridge next to a hut, Gary loaded both chambers of his shotgun and sat it on the seat next to him, while Asmani wondered off, looking for signs of life.

He returned soon after, accompanied by an elderly semi-naked man, followed by a dozen or so naked kids, cautiously staring at the Land Rover with apprehension.

The elderly man happened to be the chief and the father of Asmani's friend Goby, who was out hunting and checking traps that had been left overnight. He welcomed them and invited them to stay for as long as they needed, he even offered a hut that they could share, which Gary politely declined saying that he had bedding at the back of his Land Rover, but Asmani accepted the offer.

His friend arrived before dusk. He introduced Gary as Bwana Gazi. Goby was a very small man, who stood about five foot two inches and did not carry an ounce of fat on him. He was next in line to be chief of his people and was well respected by his tribe for being a fierce warrior and a great hunter. It was said that he could chase an antelope for days, eventually running it down until it collapsed from exhaustion.

The weather remained unchanged for the next two days, heavy rain persisted. Back in Mombasa, Karen was getting anxious as Gary was two days overdue and no contact had been made. Although her mother assured her that he was a grown man and had proven that he could take care of himself, she still insisted on calling every police post along the highway between Nairobi and Mombasa to make inquiries. Eventually being told by one of the police post that the road had been closed for several days eased her mind a little but did not stop her from worrying.

Goby came back from his hunt the next day empty-handed, rain had made hunting difficult and not possessing guns, they were using bows, poison arrows, and traps, which during wet season made hunting just about impossible.

Asmani approached Gary that afternoon seeking permission to go out and shoot an antelope as the tribe was slowly running out of food and would need him to accompany them as it was illegal for a native to carry a firearm,

At first Gary was a bit apprehensive as he had never shot an animal and did not think that he could bring himself to kill a defenceless creature, but he decided to accompany them and let Asmani do the shooting. However, he carried his gun in case it was needed and did not want to leave it unattended in the Land Rover.

That afternoon, he, Asmani, Goby and two other men left on foot to a nearby hunting ground across the river, a nicely pastured parcel of land that attracted lots of antelopes, they were told. Once there, they realised that high waters and its abundance of hungry crocodiles, made the crossing precarious, so instead, they quietly followed Goby down the side of the river into some dense vegetation. Approximately fifty metres into the bush he suddenly came to a halt and pointed straight ahead.

Through the trees stood a huge eland, the biggest of all antelopes. Gary figured it could weigh close to a ton and was not certain his rifle was powerful enough to bring down a beast of that size. Asmani was trailing a long way behind, waiting could startle the beast, so he had no other option but to try. The animal was looking away from him, giving him a sideway view, exposing its temple. Although this was the smallest target, it would be the only shot that would instantly kill the beast.

The shot was right on target, the eland went down.

Gary stood there motionless for about thirty seconds, feeling bad for having killed such a magnificent beast, while Goby and his two companions were cheering and chanting and engaging in a celebratory dance.

They cut the animal's throat and let the blood soak into the soil in a gesture of returning the animal's soul back to the earth where they believed it evolved and offering thanks to the Gods for their good fortune.

In the chant he heard the word Bwana Gazi repeated several times as they set out to butcher the beast and carry it back to camp. It took two men to carry one leg and on their return another dozen men arrived to help. Nothing from the beast was wasted, the animal was equally shared amongst their tribes, the bones would be used for soup, excess meat would be dried and preserved. Knowing that the kill was essential for the survival of the tribe gave Gary great relief in justifying his act.

On their way back to camp he noticed other smaller groups of camps dotted around the area, indicating that the tribe was well spread over a vast area and the place at which they were camped was only for the chief and his immediate family. It turned out that the chief had four wives and twenty-seven children, sixteen of them girls.

Back at the camp he was met and thanked by the chief and invited to participate in the feast that would be held that evening in thanks to their gods for having provided them with food. The meal consisted of ground maize, finely crushed and cooked into a paste called *ougali*, corn, sweet potatoes, and cassava cooked on coal. Pieces of meat were thrown onto an open fire and once retrieved, the charcoal was scraped off before consuming. Kids were walking around holding and eating half cooked pieces of meat with blood dripping over their naked bodies. A brew was made from a mixture of berries gathered by the tribe's women, then once dried, water and some kind of hops were added and left to ferment for days and eventually it turned into a strong, intoxicating drink called *dangerua*. Inside the chief's hut, men had gathered around and smoking weeds known as *Bangi*. The smell was so strong that Gary felt light headed just being in there, and after having taken a sip of the brew and inhaling the smoke from the weeds, he woke up during the night with a fierce headache and the sensation of hearing a freight train running through his head.

Chapter 19

The rain abated during the night, replaced by a clear sky displaying a magnificent moon and an abundance of stars and leaving behind at dawn an eerie thick fog with minimum visibility. Remembering the advice received from the road crew that once the rain stopped the road would be passable within a day, they decided to leave as soon as the fog lifted which was not till mid-afternoon.

Thanking Gary for providing his tribe with a kill, the chief and the medicine man came over and gave him a bracelet made from Giraffe Maine, and told him to wear on his left wrist as it would protect him from all evil spirits.

They thanked the chief for his hospitality and set out and with the road less slippery than they had experienced on the way in, they were able to reach the highway within fifteen minutes. At the junction, they turned and headed east towards the coast. On reaching the area where the trucks and graders were stuck, only two trucks remained. The two graders were cautiously attempting to smooth out the damaged parts of the highway and a sign had been posted, giving access to four wheel drive vehicles only.

They pulled in at a general store twelve miles further and fuelled up. At the telephone inside the shop, Gary booked a call to Karen at her office and being a government department the call was free. The receptionist who answered the call was the same lady he met on that first day on his arrival to Africa. She sounded relieved hearing his voice and after a short pause the call was transferred to Karen's office.

"This is a call to the Department of Internal Security," said a recorded voice. "If you are listening to this call, we strongly advise you to hang up now or there will be consequences."

Gary was dumbfounded, not realising what was going on.

There was a click from the other end, sounding like a call being terminated and the phone returned to its receiver. Gary thought that he had been cut off. Then Karen's voice burst through.

"Hello Gary, how are you and where are you?"

"What was that all about?" Gary asked in astonishment.

"The operators have a habit of listening to people's conversation," she replied. "I've been so worried about you, what happened?"

"The highway had been closed for the last three days."

"How are you?" she asked again. "You will be here tomorrow, won't you?"

"I will do my best," he replied.

"I'll have dinner ready in anticipation. I can't wait to see you," she said before hanging up.

As they drove on, they came upon countless numbers of cars, broken down, bogged, or involved in accidents, thankfully none resulting in fatal or terribly bad injuries. Forty miles further, they came to a small village called Mtito Andei, and decided to make camp for the night. Soon after, other travellers arrived and also set up camp.

Thick fog blanketed the place the following morning, preventing the sun from coming through and reducing visibility to about ten feet. Not wishing to wait any longer, as further rain was forecast, they decided to resume their journey at a much slower pace.

A few miles down the road, they came across the first previous night's mishap. A Mercedes Benz had collided with a rhinoceros. Apparently after being stunned for several minutes, the animal got up and ran off. The car however, came off second best, and was a total write off, but somehow the driver and passenger escaped with only shock and a few minor scratches.

Further along the way they came across a Volkswagen that was parked on the side of the road with all the rubber on its wheel missing. They stopped to see if they could assist but found it to be unoccupied.

Asmani assured Gary, that it was a common occurrence in Africa. If you break down, you must stay with your vehicle, otherwise the natives cut off all the rubber from the wheels to make sandals. Apparently this driver ran out of fuel, left his car unattended and took a lift to the village five miles away. On his return an hour later, he found his car completely tyre-less.

By ten o'clock a slight breeze had dispersed the fog, revealing a magnificent vista of huge plains. The dried savannah grass lands he had seen from the train on his way up was now replaced by lush, green fields with an abundance of wild life, the ever present thorn trees spreading as far as the eye could see on both sides of the highway. Although the rough divots left from the trucks made the trip slow and uncomfortable, it was compensated for by the beautiful scenery they witnessed along the way. They finally made Voi Junction by mid-afternoon, leaving them approximately eighty miles to their destination. After refuelling and some refreshment they headed off again.

Another twenty miles of slow hard going and they reached a stretch of bitumen road in a place called MacKinnon Road. The eighteen kilometre road was part of the site of a large British engineering depot built in 1947, designed to hold 200,000 tons of military stores. It was abandoned in 1950 and turned into a prison for the Mau Mau. They entered Mombasa late that day, tired and dusty from the long tedious trip. On the way, he dropped Asmani at his uncle's place on the outskirts of the town.

Karen watched in dismay as the mud-covered Land Rover pulled up in her driveway. In disbelief she watched a muddy and unshaven person push open the driver's door and extricate himself from the confines of the vehicle. Overjoyed and relieved to see him, she ran and threw her arms around him and at the same time exclaimed; "How the hell did you get here in that?"

Karen's mother came out to meet him and straight away asked if he would like a shower, which he gladly accepted. From the back of the vehicle he picked up his mud-covered travel case and carried it to the spare room. He showered, shaved, washed his hair with the shampoo

Karen had provided and came out looking fresh and clean, dressed in a cream pair of pants and a blue short-sleeved shirt.

As he entered the lounge Karen came over to him, gave him a hug and said, "I've been so worried about you, especially these last few days, that I have hardly had a decent night's sleep. Now that you are here, I should sleep like a baby."

A sumptuous roast dinner had been prepared by Karen's mum. For the evening meal, he participated in a glass of wine over dinner, they had coffee on the front veranda overlooking the harbour entrance and although exhausted, they sat and talked till close to midnight discussing plans for locating his Dad, and of her being contacted by her boss, Anthony Phillips insisting she give him every possible assistance in his quest.

He told her how he and Anthony got acquainted, about his stay with him and his family in Nairobi, of finding him easy going and friendly, contrary to Karen's opinion, who found him to be a little abrupt and even rude at times.

"I have to admit though, that his attitude changed greatly when he found out that I knew and helped you while in Mombasa on your arrival. He must think very highly of you," Karen said.

They both slept in till late morning and being a Saturday, Karen did not have to work.

Gary went out to his Land Rover to retrieve some paper work and to his surprise found the vehicle had been washed by the Shamba boy, with instruction from Karen's mum before she left for golf. Once washed, it did not look dilapidated at all, as previously thought by Karen. It was altogether a good and sound vehicle, well set up for what he needed it for.

Karen had to call in at her office before noon to pick up a file she was working on. She asked him to accompany her and while in town they would have lunch at the Tudor House restaurant in the town centre. Once again they ran into more of Karen's friends.

From the restaurant they called on Asmani at his uncle's place to make sure he was okay. He still kept insisting that he would not be going home until he had helped Gary locate his father.

"I don't think that you're going to get him to change his mind," Karen told him. "So you'd better accept his help, he could possibly be very handy, and a great help to you."

Gary made a deal with Asmani, saying that he would gladly accept his help, but as he had other business to attend to in Mombasa, he would not be ready to leave for another week at least. So he would be happy to see Asmani go home and visit his family and return in a week's time. Asmani agreed to the deal and made arrangement to meet the following Monday. They shook hands on that, and Gary left.

Chapter 20

Karen decided to take the following Monday and Tuesday off. She spent a few hours on Sunday working on the file she had picked up from her office the day before but she wouldn't tell Gary what the content was. All secretive stuff, Gary thought.

On Monday morning, Karen returned the file to the safe in her office and then rang head office in Nairobi to advise them of her absence. Within minutes, her boss Anthony was on the phone asking if she was ill. She explained to him that she wanted to give Gary some help accessing his father's bank records and any other legal step required, hoping that her credentials would help.

"Better than that," Anthony said. "That young man has done his share for this country, so forget about taking leave. Open a file on his father, mark it confidential. I'll issue you with a code, let your office know that you are on an assignment, take the two days and let me know if you need more time, keep me posted, and take care." He hung up the phone.

Karen put the phone down, feeling stunned. Concerned, Gary asked her what the problem was. She related the conversation to him. She then called her deputy, a man in his forties, and told him that she would be away on an assignment for two days. During her absence, all inquiries were to be directed to head office in Nairobi. Then she and Gary left.

In silence, they drove out in her departmental car as she took a moment to reflect on the conversation.

"Is Anthony for real?" she asked.

"Why do you ask?" Gary said.

"Well, he just gave me a couple of days off to assist you."

"What's wrong with that?"

"Nothing," she replied. "It's just not like him to do that." She shook her head in disbelief and laughed.

Their first call was his father's previous apartment, a three-bedroom serviced apartment in an affluent suburb overlooking the water. Gary's letter was sent to this address on the day of his arrival. The caretaker told them that Gary's father had left money with her to redirect his mail to the post office box, but there had been no mail for well over six months and he had not made contact with her since.

They stopped at a coffee shop in the centre of town called the Copper Kettle. Karen dug out an empty file from her bag. There were a few plain sheets of paper inside and they prepared a list of places they would have to visit, starting with the bank, then the department of motor transport, lands department, internal revenue, taxation office and so on.

Barclays Bank, situated in the lower part of the town was their first stop. At the reception counter they asked to see the manager. The receptionist was about to ask the purpose of their inquiry, when Karen gave her one of those looks that sent her rushing to her manager's office. The manager was a little man with two yellow nicotine stained fingers on his right hand, obviously a chain smoker. He arrived promptly and introduced himself and although they had never met, he knew of Karen and her department.

She asked for the banking records for Gary's father going back for two years.

"That may take a while," he told her.

Karen looked at her watch, and said, "We'll be back in fifteen minutes to collect it and then we'll need your kind assistance with some other minor details."

She turned and walked out and like a lost sheep, Gary followed.

The records were ready and waiting when they returned. They were escorted directly to the Manager's office. Karen pushed an ashtray that was filled with cigarette butts sitting on the desk away from her and the manager must have got the message. He quickly moved and placed it on a shelf behind his desk.

Karen compared the signature from the cheque to the specimen, and found it to be matching. In the banking records, the place where the cheques had been cashed was listed. The bank account was very healthy. No wonder the manager was guarding it so closely, obviously not wanting to lose it, Gary thought. He soon realised that his Dad was a wealthy person.

The manager finally asked the reason for the investigation. Karen told him that it was a probable missing person and that Gary was his son looking for him. The manager seemed relieved.

Their next stop was the Department of Motor Transport. Although the insurance and registration were all up to date, it gave them no help as his year old Peugeot was registered under a post office box number. A residential address was not required to register a vehicle in East Africa.

Upon visiting the post office, they found that the few letters in the box were less than two months old and Gary's letter that was written on the day of his arrival was not amongst them.

His father's personal tax record showed that his business dealings were mainly carried out in the town of Tanga in the state of Tanganyika, eighty miles away, and all records showed that his taxes were up to date. They decided to visit the town of Tanga the following day.

They left early in the morning and took the Likoni Ferry Across to the mainland on the southern side and drove the eighty dusty miles in three hours.

They arrived at the Tanga Lands Department soon after opening and again, Karen's internal security badge proved invaluable. They soon established that Gary's father owned a large cashew plantation, twenty miles from the town, currently leased to a pastoral company and managed by an Indian manager.

They decided to pay him a visit. He was at first a bit apprehensive about divulging any information and wanted to know if they had a court order. Karen was getting a bit frustrated with him, but explained that Gary was the owner's son, and he had been reported missing. He eventually began to show more cooperation.

His company had a five year lease on the place he told them, with the option of extending the lease to two more terms. The contract was drawn up by Gary's father's solicitor in Tanga, and their solicitor was holding their contract. The lease payment was being made monthly into an account at Barclays Bank in Mombasa. He gave them the name and number in which the account was held, they thanked him and left.

Next they called on his accountant who confirmed doing his tax the year before, and as this year's returns were not due for a few more months he had not been contacted. He also confirmed his contact number as the post office box in Mombasa.

Gary was feeling uneasy. Something was not adding up, he told Karen. If there was another account, why hadn't the bank manager informed them?

Who was collecting his mail?

Had his father received the letter he sent?

How was he surviving?

No great sum of money had been withdrawn anytime in the past year and only two withdrawals made in the last four months.

Karen offered to call the bank manager, but Gary suggested that they should personally visit him.

After a quick bite for lunch, they started the drive back to Mombasa.

"I'm very fortunate to have met you," Gary said to Karen. "I really appreciate your help."

She noticed a small quaver in his voice.

"You must also thank your friend Anthony," she replied.

He nodded his head in acknowledgement.

Mr Cool must be human after all, Karen thought, as they drove in silence for the next five miles. *You are worth every minute of my time. Beside that's what friends are for.* She looked at him and winked.

Gary's Father purchased a ten acre property with an old magnificent homestead thirty miles out of Mombasa. A property he had been trying to buy for years, but the owners never wanted to part with, eventually had come up for sale a few days before he was due to leave for his trip, with plan to renovate on his return. He had used all his spare money obtained from his sisal estate dividend to pay for it

Josef stayed and looked after the property, and part of his job was to go to Mombasa once a month and collect the mail from the post office, and kept in the safe until his return. At first he was collecting them once a month, but as the letter decreased he opted to collect them once every two to three months.

Chapter 21

Karen returned to work on Wednesday morning while Gary visited some of his father's old friends in the hope of getting other information that may have recently surfaced, but the result proved negative.

At the Central Police Station in the main street, he introduced himself and explained the purpose of his visit. He was directed to see a detective at the Crime Investigation Branch and after a short wait he was ushered to an office where he met a middle-aged man who said he was the senior detective in the station.

To Gary's surprise, a missing person's file had been activated on his Dad. The detective withdrew the folder from the filing cabinet and placed it on his desk but was astonished when he opened the folder and found that the file and its contents had been removed and replaced by a note stating that internal security had taken possession of the contents.

"That's very unusual," the detective said. "Was your father working for the government?"

"Not that I am aware of," Gary replied.

"I'm sorry," the detective said, "but until I get the file back, my hands are tied. I am truly sorry."

Gary drove over to Karen's office and told her about his meeting with the detective.

"I have the file here," Karen said. "I made them re-open the case a month after you were drafted. That's how I got the information about the cheques being cashed. I requested it last week after talking to Anthony, to see if any new evidence had surfaced. Sometimes these guys get information, enter it in the file, put it away then forget about it for months on end, always claiming to be too busy, but somehow they're never too busy to attend happy hour at the club."

"What exactly is your Department's role?" Gary asked.

"The role of Internal Security is to investigate corruption in public service sectors," she said. "But now it also includes Intelligence, and Security in both the Kenya Police and the Regiments. I talked to Anthony this morning. He has asked me to accompany you to the village near Voi where the cheques were cashed, and interview the people involved. If it's okay with you, we could leave Friday morning, book in at the Tsavo Safari Lodge for the weekend and if we have time, maybe visit the National Park and return home on Sunday."

"That sounds wonderful," Gary replied. "We can use my Land Rover."

"We sure can," Karen said, not wanting to offend him, then after a slight pause, said, "The department just took delivery of two brand new Land Rovers. It would look more official if we use one of them."

Although Gary agreed that it was a good idea, he didn't let on. Instead he arranged to meet for drinks after work at the Splendid Hotel roof garden. The eight story hotel was situated in the centre of the town and from the jungle decor of the roof garden bar and restaurant, it had great views of the township and its night lights, making it a popular meeting place.

As Karen's mother was away for a couple of days visiting friends, they decided to stay and have dinner at the restaurant.

Back home later that evening, being one of those Mombasa hot, still and humid weeks, where temperatures constantly remained well into the high twenties during the night, sitting on the veranda directly under a ceiling fan that was slowly rotating helped give them some comfort, while looking out across the harbour entrance, admiring the effervescent reflexion from street lights bouncing across the water, only to be disturbed by the washes from the ferry as they moved across the harbour. They were so relaxed that Gary for once actually finished the glass of wine that he had carefully nursed for most of the evening, while Karen was on her second.

She was lying across the cane lounge with her head on his chest, attempting to match his heart beat to the tempo of the music, when without warning she impulsively jumped up and passionately kissed him. He was caught by surprise, a moment he had only dreamed about and at first he was not sure whether to respond, but passion soon took its course and he responded hungrily. He felt like pinching himself to make sure that he was not dreaming but realised that it was real.

He carried her to his bedroom and gently laid her on the bed while admiring her beauty and looking deeply into her eyes, whispered," you are so beautiful." She responded with more kisses, as they slowly undressed each other, he was so gentle with his touch, that she completely surrendered her body to his desire. Conscious of his above average size manhood, and not wanting to cause her any physical pain, he entered her with ultra-gentleness, something that had never happened with any of the other girls he had previously been with, although he was always known to be gentle in his love making.

The morning found them entwined in each other's arms.

"That will save us the extra room on our weekend," she said in a soft voice.

He responded with a gentle loving kiss.

As she left for work some time later, he sat on the veranda with a cup of coffee and watched her drive down the road until her car disappeared out of sight. He showered, dressed and drove to the bank to withdraw some funds for the trip. The bank manager spotted him at the counter, and asked him to his office for a chat and while in there, had coffee served by one of his assistants.

"After having enquired about the progress in locating his father," he said, "we know that some of the investments on term deposit were about to mature. The bank will need authority to reinvest and so far, the letters written to your father at the post office box have neither been answered or returned."

"It hadn't been picked up either, going by the last time I checked," Gary said.

"I will have to contact our legal department to see how we best go about it," the manager said. "Being the next of kin, you may have to make that decision. The only other alternative is to roll them over for another period."

Gary left and drove to the Copper Kettle Restaurant where he was meeting Karen for lunch. Watching her walking in, brought on the desire to run up and grab hold of her. Somehow the uniform kept him at bay.

He was telling her about his recent meeting with the bank manager and what he'd been told about his father's finances, when the waiter arrived with the lunch menu. Gary felt as famished as the day he arrived in Mombasa and ordered the biggest meal on the menu, the famous mixed grill, but this time asked them to hold back the lamb fries. Although not known to being a great eater, he devoured a large portion of it. Karen on the other hand, settled for chicken served on a green salad.

That evening and the next was spent quietly in their individual beds, as Karen's mother had returned from her little holiday.

Chapter 22

As dawn broke that morning, they were well on their way, heading west to the town of Voi. The morning sun greeted them by forcing its rays through the fog onto the shimmering wet leaves and spider webs stretching along both sides of the highway, resembling delicate lace, with beads of dew glistening like diamonds as it welcomed the new day. A few miles further along found them driving on the twelve miles bitumen stretch of road that went past the township of Mackinnon Road.

Back on the dirt road they encountered a road gang who had closed a section of the highway that had been damaged during the previous heavy rain and a few miles further, a grader operator was frantically grading parts that had been badly grooved by truck wheels, turning it nice and smooth but terribly dusty. In fact it was so bad that they had to stop and let the dust settle every time they came across another vehicle.

They arrived at Voi Safari Lodge, at the entrance of the National Park around 10.00am, deposited their luggage in the two adjoining rooms that had previously been booked through her office under their individual names. After an early lunch, they left for the little village of Mwatate, situated at the base of the Taita hills on the Voi to Arusha Road eighteen miles away.

The general store where the cheques had been cashed was also an agency for Barclays Bank, local post office and the telephone exchange depot.

"That could be very helpful," Karen assured him. "If he is in this area he may even be using this place to make his calls and post his letters."

Once inside, she asked to speak to the store owner or manager.

They were greeted by a middle aged Indian man who came out of his office and asked how he could be of assistance to them. She showed him her identity and a copy of the cheque and asked if he remembered cashing it. He studied it closely then went to his office and returned with a ledger. In it was the date the cheque was cashed and the name of the person who cashed it. Karen was impressed.

"The person who cashed the cheque is an employee who works on a nearby Sisal Estate," said the manager. "I know him well." He gave them directions to the Estate.

Karen then showed him a photo of Gary's father and asked whether he knew him or had seen him in the area.

"Not personally," he replied, "but I know of him by reputation through his help and generosity to the locals."

The lady in the post office who also ran the telephone exchange was of no help, she was too busy plugging and unplugging cords into the control box.

They left, got back in the car and set off, following the man's directions.

At the Sisal Estate, Karen showed her badge to the operations manager who directed them to the man they were looking for, the one who had cashed the cheque. They located him at the factory. He told them that he knew Gary's father rather well, he sold him the Land Rover just over six months ago for the sum of four hundred pounds (eight thousand shillings) and was given two cheques, one he could cash immediately, and the other post-dated by two months.

"Why would a man with loads of money in the bank do something like that?"Karen asked.

"If you knew him, you would understand," the man replied. "He is a very cautious man, and if the car turned out to be a lemon, he would have stopped the other cheque."

What a shrewd man, Karen thought. "How did he know that your vehicle was for sale, and where was it advertised?" she asked.

"At the general store here and at Voi," he replied. "Look," he went on to say. "A few friends of mine knew that my car was up for sale, I've been trying to sell it for a while, as my job here comes with a car. One of them could have mentioned it to him."

"Who drove him here to pick up the car?" Gary asked.

"The local mechanic from Voi, an Indian man came with him, checked the vehicle out and he drove it back."

They left with the car's details and registration number, make, model and colour and headed back to Voi to talk to the mechanic. He confirmed the man's version, that he went up with Bwana Maxi to inspect the Land Rover then drove it back to his garage and serviced it. The vehicle was picked up two days later by Bwana Maxi's house boy Josef, and the bill was settled in cash.

"Can you describe what Bwana Maxi looks like?" Karen asked. He gave her an exact description of him and when she produced the photo, he confirmed that it was him, but commented that the photograph must have been taken a while back as he was much older in reality.

From there they drove to the local police headquarters that managed the entire Taveta / Taita district. Karen went in to hand in details of the Land Rover to the officer in charge and have it kept on file.

Dressed in civilian clothes, she made her way to the Voi Police Station Reception area. Gary thought that she looked so elegant and beautiful and walked in with an air of grace that one could only marvel at. But underneath all that beauty was a woman with enough determination and power to cut anyone down to size in seconds.

A white officer came out, displaying a playboy look and asked, "What can I do for you, beautiful?"

She looked at him without batting an eye, and said, "May I see the officer in charge please?"

He stood there and looked at her.

"Are you the person in charge?" she demanded again.

"I could be," he replied, and again asked, "What can I do for you, sweetheart?"

Displaying one of the pleasant, yet 'I will tear you apart' smiles, Karen replied, "I am not your sweetheart. I have politely asked to see the officer in charge. Now, can you please get him for me?"

By this time her sweet smile had disappeared and her official look and tone of voice, had taken over.

He stood there for a moment pretending not to have heard.

She looked him straight in the eye, and in a low intimidating voice, said, "You seem to have a problem understanding me, officer. I am asking you in plain English to get me the person in charge. Now will you be a good boy, run along and get him for me, please."

The officer's face had turned bright red, either through high blood pressure or by being belittled in front of his work colleagues.

Gary wondering what was taking her so long, entered the reception area where another officer was moving towards him to offer his assistance, but stopped suddenly when Karen said in a firm voice, "He is with me."

The officer escorted them to the regional Superintendent's office, knocked on the door and opened it, saying to the unseen man inside, "Visitors to see you, sir."

Karen and Gary walked in and the officer left. Seated behind a desk was an officer with the rank badges of a Superintendent. He rose as the visitors entered and his face betrayed the admiration he felt for Karen.

"Superintendent Jackson," he said. "How can I help you, madam?"

"Inspector Karen Willis, Internal Security," she said and produced her warrant card. Jackson blinked but showed no further reaction, handing back her card.

"And what are you doing here, Inspector Willis?"

"A missing person," said Karen, handing the Superintendent a piece of paper on which was the make, colour and registration number of the Land Rover in question. "I would like you to put a call to all your vehicles patrolling the area to watch for that particular vehicle. If it is located, order your officers to apprehend and report to me immediately at the Tsavo Safari Lodge. That is where I will be staying for the next two days, and after that at my office in Mombasa.

She started to make her exit, then made a sudden stop, turned and faced the Superintendent and said, "The officer that assisted me, would you kindly forward his name, rank and number to my office, as I am putting him on report." Before the officer could reply, she turned and left his office.

The Superintendent called the officer in and enquired the cause of Karen's anger? The junior officer explained the incident, stating that he was simply having a joke with her.

"You imbecile," the Superintendent said. "I cannot believe you said that to an Inspector in Internal Security."

The other man looked frightened. "I didn't know that's what she was. She didn't show me any identification."

The Superintendent looked furious. "This is going to look bad on me," he said. "Whatever happened, she is putting you on report. I can't offer you any help with that, nor would I want to get involved either. The only advice I can give you is that since she'll be staying at the resort for a couple of days, crawl there on your knees if you have to, and try to apologise. I would not do it today though, as she is one pissed off lady, with enough power to drag your ass to the NFD. [1] Go home and pray that she calms down by tomorrow. Now instead of being home with my family, I

---

[1] (Northern Frontier District) - *situated on the edge of the desert bordering Somalia, temperatures drop as low as minus five degrees during the night and reach as high as mid-forties during the day. It is not a popular place to be stationed, troops are sent there to do border protection.*

have to stay here and make a full report on your stupidity to cover my own arse and maybe start looking for your replacement, because that is exactly what is going to happen. Now get out of my office."

Chapter 23

Back at the resort, Karen had settled down. Gary ordered her a Martini and a lemon squash for himself. They sat on the balcony overlooking the park, watching herds of antelope frolicking around the water hole that was also being visited by a senate of baboons.

"What happened back there?" he asked.

She looked at him and with her beautiful smile said, "Nothing much." After taking another sip of her Martini, she continued. "I just cannot tolerate stupidity. I suppose I over-reacted. This guy's attitude was wrong, he's a public servant and should show more respect. There's no place for people like him in the force."

Gary understood the reaction of a young police officer stationed in the bush and suddenly seeing a pretty girl at the counter. He certainly had been disrespectful but Gary was not sure he'd be so angry. But in the mood she was in, he was not prepared to deliberate any further on the subject.

That evening they drove to a well-known observation point approximately five miles into the park where herds of elephants and other animals congregated at dusk for their daily drink. From a big rocky outlook on the western side above the water hole, a safe enclosed area had been set for tourists to view and take photos.

The 10,000 square mile park was opened in the coastal province on the edge of the Taita District in 1948. This semi-arid and savannah grass land, has the two rivers running through it, the Tsavo and the Athi that eventually flow into a single river called the Galana and finally out to sea near the town of Lamu. Contrary to what the train guard had previously told him, hunting was actually permitted in the National Park under strict license.

Back at the lodge he sat quietly and reflected on the day's event, the chances of locating his father, what was his next move, and where.

Karen on the other hand was more optimistic. "Let's put this in perspective," she said. "Your Dad has been missing for well over nine months, he bought the car from the man at the sisal plantation just over six months ago, if what he said is true, and I believe it is, the date on the cheque confirms it, the signature appears to be genuine, as far as we know from medical records, he is in good health, has had his vehicle serviced here and he is known to the locals. So I strongly believe that your Dad is alive and living somewhere in this area.

"The reason for his silence is still the mystery we must unearth. I strongly feel that the place you must concentrate on looking for him is actually here in the Taita Hills district. As far as money goes, he has proven to be a smart man, he could have enough cash stashed away to last him a lifetime. I also believe that if for some unknown reason he wants to disappear for a while, he won't be easy to find, even with all the resources we now have on hand."

Gary reflected on what Karen had said, and agreed that it made perfect sense. It also gave him further hope, having been reassured that his father was alive and he was getting closer to finding him.

The one thing that he could not understand was why would his father who had everything, want to withdraw from society? It just did not add up. However for now he felt relieved, and was going to enjoy his time in the company of his new-found love.

After dinner, they sat and listened to an African band playing local Africans and blues music, they held hands, stole the occasional kisses, laughed and danced till late. On the way to their room as they walked past the resort rose garden, he plucked a rose bud, and placed it in her hair, while giving her a gentle kiss. They spent the rest of the night exploring each other's body, kissed and made love till exhaustion overcame them and they fell into a deep sleep.

Totally naked, relaxed and famished, they were awakened by chirping birds in nearby acacias and greeted by rays of the morning sun filtering through their window blinds.

Karen rang room service and ordered breakfast, a serve each of bacon and eggs, toast, marmalade, jam, coffee, orange juice and the morning paper. She wrapped herself in the bed sheet, went and opened the door, when it arrived. Gary's eyes followed her every move, he could not stop admiring her, she looked so elegant even wrapped in a bed sheet, he thought.

They decided to spend the rest of the day exploring the National Park in an attempt to see how many different animals they would spot along their trip around. At the reception desk they ordered a picnic lunch basket, included in it were mixed sandwiches, a thermos of coffee, two bottles of water, and a selection of tropical fruits, with instructions for it to be delivered to their vehicle.

Through the park, their time was mainly taken by scrutinizing the number plates on every white Land Rover they encountered, instead of identifying animal species.

They stopped for lunch in a fenced rocky outcrop picnic area next to a spring where a number of vehicles were already parked. They ate their lunch in the comfort of the Land Rover, avoiding being attacked by flies.

Fascinated by a couple of water birds that were aggressively chasing each other up and down the water's edge, Karen, who was eating and enjoying a delicious apple, got out of the vehicle, went and sat on a rock at the edge of the fence where she had a better view of the two birds. Out of nowhere a tiny little monkey appeared, grabbed the apple from Karen's hand and like a flash was back sitting in the tree branch, watching her while eating the apple.

Gary tried very hard not to laugh, but the look of disbelief on Karen face was too much and he couldn't hold back.

It was fairly late in the afternoon when they finally arrived back at the lodge. Waiting at the reception was a letter addressed to Karen, marked private and confidential. She asked the receptionist if she knew the origin of the letter, and was told that a police officer had delivered it. She opened the letter and found it to be an apology from the officer she had a run in with the day before, stating that his Superintendent would verify that he was a good officer and obviously had a brain failure that day. Karen murmured something, shook her head and put the letter in her bag.

They went to their room to freshen up before making their way to the observation deck that overlooked the water hole. Gary ordered a bottle of white wine and two glasses, sat at a table on the southern side of the deck away from the afternoon tourist crowds. Gary was starting to enjoy the occasional glasses of wine, he even warned Karen that he was well on his way to becoming an alcoholic and she would have to accept the blame.

They had been there for well over an hour and were deeply concentrating on a couple of baby elephants having a wonderful time squirting water from their trunks at one another, when they heard footsteps approaching from behind the hedge that separated their table from view of the bar area, then a male voice.

"Hello inspector, nice to see you again."

They both turned at once and saw the Superintendent.

"My wife and I would be honoured if you both could join us," he said.

"That's very kind of you, Superintendent," said Karen, turning to Gary to seek his approval.

"I see that like us, you prefer to be away from the crowd," said the Superintendent. "Our table is also in a secluded corner."

"I must say you are very observant, sir," Karen replied and rose to her feet. Garry did the same and the officer led them to his table.

There, they were introduced to his wife who turned out to be a very nice lady. She and Karen got on tremendously well, they talked about places they both knew in England, chatted about fashions, travels, women's topics in general, while the Superintendent and Gary exchanged fishing tales, a topic Gary was well attuned to and passionate about.

Seeing that they had a lot in common, and were very interested in knowing more about the Seychelles and possibly other reasons relating to Karen's confrontation with one of his officers, the Superintendent insisted that they join them for dinner. Karen however, was hesitant at first, saying that she did not want to impose on their privacy, but through the Superintendent's continuous insistence, she eventually succumbed to his request.

During dinner, Karen took the opportunity to explain Gary's situation and the quest to find his father. The Superintendent offered to personally assist Gary while in his district. Knowing how complicated things could get, especially in dealing with government departments, Gary gratefully accepted his offer.

During dinner the Superintendent again apologised to Karen about his officer's behaviour.

"He's a good officer, I really don't know what came over him," the Superintendent said.

Karen thought for a while, and then said, "He has written a letter of apology but since I have already written a report, I will have to discuss it with my superior."

Although he was well aware that there she was the most senior person in her department in Mombasa, the Superintendent did not pursue the matter any further.

"And if I don't press charges it will be thanks to you, Superintendent," Karen concluded.

With that, he seemed relieved, and also flattered.

Karen was pleased with the outcome, confident that Gary would get the help he needed. They both enjoyed the company of the Superintendent and his wife. He was a jovial person, especially after a few drinks under his belt and had some fantastic stories to tell. They talked till late and Gary was getting a little light headed on his third glass of wine, while the Superintendent was on his third or fourth bottle. Eventually Karen got up excused herself saying that it had been a long and tiring day, they both thanked the Superintendent and his wife for the wonderful evening and offered to return the favour whenever they visited Mombasa.

They slept till late the next day, left the resort around 11.00 am and slowly drove back to Mombasa with plans to stop and have lunch at the well-known White Horse Inn Hotel in Mackinnon Road.

The owners, an elderly ex-army colonel and his wife had opened the hotel after his retirement from the service. During the military occupation of Mackinnon Road, it became a popular place that was well patronised by high ranking army personnel.

When the army base finally closed in 1950, it became known as a stopover place where exaggerated travel encounter stories were exchanged between travellers on their road between Nairobi and Mombasa. Displayed on the wall in the lounge area were hand written stories of some of the most gruesome tales and legends.

Gary and Karen had just ordered lunch, when a huge left hand drive American car drove in with the sound of gears crunching as it headed straight for the largest Acacia tree standing in the front yard that had a large *no parking* sign displayed in front of it. The car collided head on with the tree, and came to a sudden stop. Gary was up about to run out and assist when a lady called out that he was okay. The door opened and out stepped a six foot plus elderly gentleman, dragging out a half filled basket of vegetables that was probably full before the impact. A young African boy dressed in a white uniform who was standing nearby and undeterred by the commotion, ran and opened the rear door and foraged around the back of the car picking up the vegetables that had been spilt on the floor and under the seats.

Gary must have looked concerned. To put his mind at rest, a lady saying she was the elderly gentlemen's daughter came over and assured him that what he had just witnessed was a weekly occurrence. Her father's car brakes had been inoperable for well over a year now as he had not been able to procure any parts for it. Until about a year ago, he had been using the hand brake, but when that failed he opted for the tree. There was also a tree that he used at the market place, she said and it too had a *no parking* sign displayed in front.

It took a while for Karen and Garry to stop laughing at the episode,

They arrived back in Mombasa late that afternoon, and called on Asmani to make sure he was back from visiting his family. They found him sitting on the front step talking to his uncle. He greeted them with a big grin displaying his white teeth as they drove in and told them that he had arrived back early that morning.

"I somehow trust this fellow," Karen told Gary as they drove away. "He seems a very trust worthy person. I will feel better knowing that he is travelling with you."

Chapter 24

Early Monday morning Gary called on Asmani to update him with their plans.

"Have you talked to any of the servants employed at his previous address?" Asmani asked.

"No," Gary replied. "I have only spoken to the landlady."

"Well," said Asmani, "get me a recent photo of him, and I will go around the neighbourhood and make some inquiries."

They met later that morning. Asmani had news that Gary's Dad was known to the servants as Bwana Maxi, a very kind man who treated everyone no matter what creed or colour with total respect. His House Boy was a man from the Taita Hills named Josef. The staff believed that Josef went with him when he left, confirming the mechanic's story.

Gary thanked Asmani for his effort, and made plans to leave for the Taita Hills the following morning. They spent the rest of day getting supplies and packing up the Land Rover.

That evening he related the day's events to Karen and she totally agreed that Asmani talking to the natives was a great idea and that they should continue using Bwana Maxi as his name in their investigation.

"I told you he was smarter than the average," she said with a giggle.

The next morning Gary was packed and on his way out of town, stopped to pick Asmani up from his uncle's place, packed his belongings in the back of the Land Rover and was soon heading out of town along the causeway.

They arrived at Voi police headquarters around 10.30 am. Gary went in to see if the Superintendent was in his office to tell him that he would be in the district for possibly a couple of weeks, searching for his Dad.

Not certain if the reception would be as warm as when they last met, he cautiously approached his office and was somehow surprised by the friendly greetings he received and the continuous offer of any help needed. The Superintendent also told him that since he was still in the regiment reserve, he was entitled to use his credentials, as any other police officer, in obtaining information or help and even the power to arrest anyone found creating an offence, of which Gary was not aware, and should he need further assistance to call him personally, day or night.

Feeling more confident about the task, Gary and Asmani continued on their way. At the Voi junction, they turned left on the road that headed towards the town of Arusha in the state of Tanganyika.

The Taita district consists of three tribes, the Taita, Segalla and the Taveta, all sharing similar languages. They apparently moved to the area from the southern parts of Africa hundreds of years ago and settled in the rich agricultural land of the Taita hills and the Tsavo hunting ground. However, on the flat land they clashed heavily with the Maasai tribe, who grazed their cattle on the Tsavo plains. To avoid further conflicts they retreated into the Hills. They are a peaceful people, mostly Christians now, who cultivate their land and grow corn, cassava, beans and sweet potatoes.

They stopped outside the general store in the village of Mwatate, where he and Karen had visited the previous Friday. While Gary waited in the car, Asmani mingled and talked to several natives who were hanging around the village shops and the local market that was being held in the park next door. He showed them the photo he had of Bwana Maxi and also asked about Josef. The only positive information he returned with, was that many white men live in the Taita hills, either married or simply living with black mistresses, but no one matched the photo or description of Bwana Maxi. The picture was taken several years ago, and he could very well look so different now. Also, Josef was a very common name in the district. In the short time he spent around the village he came across eight different Josefs.

They decided to head for the Taita hills, and somehow visit all the white people living there, with the knowledge that it would not be an easy task as it covered a very large mountainous area without road names or maps.

The climb to the top was long, narrow and treacherous. Vision through the thick cloud was down to a few feet. Asmani had to get out of the car and walk ahead with a kerosene lamp, while Gary followed closely behind in the Land Rover as they zigzagged their way up the hill at less than normal walking pace. The incline at some spots was up to seventeen degrees. Lucky not to have encountered another vehicle coming from the opposite direction, they finally broke through the cloud as they neared the plateau two hours later.

In the village they came across a police post, which neither of them knew existed. Gary went in and introduced himself. It was being manned by two Askaries, who somehow did not seem deterred by his presence in the area and the reception was more as if he had been expected. Gary suspected that they might have been informed of his likely presence by the Voi police , even though they gave no indication of such.

Being a white officer, although in the reserve, automatically made him their superior and was treated as such, something he strongly detested. He was given accommodation in a one room bed sitter used by white officers on their visit to the area and Asmani was given a bunk with the two Askaries at their quarters. Gary assured them that his visit was of a personal nature, and that they should be running their station as normal. They still sought his approval and advice on every matter.

The two Askaries were well aware of the many white men residing in the hills that had taken up with black mistresses.

They also told Gary about the nearby location of a large Mission, with a Monastery and Nunnery, which was also a sanctuary for people with other problems. It was well patronised by many white men and women, sometimes staying for long periods of time. It catered for people with mental stress, alcohol problems and those seeking salvation. Gary told them he would visit the mission the following day and would need one of them to accompany him, while Asmani stayed back and continued with his inquiries at the village.

Early the following day, they drove into the parking area at the front of the huge mission perched on a hill top overlooking the beautiful vast landscape below. It was a place where novices came to study and take their vows when becoming nuns.

The local police had told Gary that the mission consisted of several individual buildings, separated from one another. They were Nunnery, Monastery, Church, Bakery, Priest Quarters, wine making areas and the cellars. Gary did not detect any vineyards on his drive to the mission, so he therefore suspected that the grapes could be grown elsewhere and transported in.

At the reception he was met by a young nun displaying a strong accent, either Irish or Scottish, he found it hard to distinguish. She could or would not divulge any information about the mission, but offered to get the Mother Superior. The name Mother Superior sent shivers down his spine, remembering the many encounters and confrontations he'd had in the past involving the Mother Superior in the Seychelles girls' dormitory at the boarding school that was run by the nuns.

He asked the young nun whether a priest would be a more appropriate person to talk to, in hope that she would be in agreement, but his question was dismissed with a smile.

"Mother Superior is the right person you need to speak to," said the young woman and quickly excused herself.

Gary was contemplating a quick exit when the door opened and a middle aged lady dressed in a Nun's habit walked in and ushered him to her office with a sweet smile. She was nothing like he had expected and his fear quickly abated. He told her about his missing Dad but he was somehow hesitant to give his full name in case his school history had been documented and circulated around many convents around the Indian Ocean. Since the Mother Superior did not seem perturbed after hearing his name, he realised that he had over reacted.

"Of course, you understand that if he was here, I would have to get his permission to give out any information," she said.

"I understand," said Gary.

They sat and talked for well over half an hour and he left with the knowledge that his father was definitely not at the mission, and his view of Mothers Superior completely altered.

Back at the village, Asmani's interviews with the natives had proven fruitless apart from information and direction of four places where white men and their black mistresses resided. He also established that they have been there for a long time, erasing the possibilities of Bwana Maxi being one of them.

The first place they came to after an hour's drive was an old dilapidated shack surrounded by a makeshift fence constructed from tree branches entwined together. In an old weather-beaten, out of shape armchair, secured by strings of sisal fibres, sat a half-naked, dirty, bearded old man, enjoying the warmth of the midday sun while constantly puffing on a pipe and exhaling smoke at intervals as if copying the puff of a steam train and in the meantime sending out a smell very different from that of tobacco.

From a distance Gary could not make out whether he was a white or not, but as he got closer, realised that he was actually white but the effect of sun, red volcanic dirt and lack of a wash had given him the dark complexion. He did not make any attempt to get out of his chair and greet him as he approached. The man answered Gary's initial questions in a strong Boer accent. Gary decided that he either had very little to say or could not be bothered holding a conversation and decided to drive on. On their way out, they spotted a few half caste naked kids playing near a stream and they too looked wild and dirty.

Driving back, they came to a junction. The Askari told him that both the tracks went to the village and since they had used the top track on their way in, Gary decided to return on the lower one. A few miles further down, they came across a well maintained property with recently painted white wooden fences and a majestic entry gate.

Ignoring the "strictly no entry" sign, Gary turned into it. About half a mile into the lane, they came to a secluded orchard being tended by half a dozen or so native workers. The place was so well maintained and set at the base of a majestic mountain using it as its backdrop and so creating the perfect scenery. A stream running past a few yards from the residence provided them with fresh water and the constant sound of the flow of water gave a sense of serenity. The house was constructed in a hexagon shape, with wrap-around verandas and built with logs and a stone fireplace in the centre; the logs were stained in grey giving it a natural antique look. From Gary's perspective, the only thing against it was the remote location, but once here, it would be a perfect place to relax and unwind. He got out of the vehicle to look at the house more clearly.

Gary fell into a world of his own admiring the place, and he failed at first to hear himself being greeted by a well-dressed African man. Garry introduced himself and showed his police reserve card. The man told him that the place was owned by a white businessman and his wife who used it as their retreat once a month. Having been their long-time employee from their residence in Mombasa, he was sent here to manage the place during their absence. Gary was very impressed with the homestead and would have loved to have been able to spend more time looking around, but as he was quickly running out of day light, he thanked the man and was about to drive out when he suddenly remembered his reason for coming to the property. He asked about Bwana Maxi but again received a negative reply.

In an attempt to visit the other three places in the company of Asmani, Gary set out again early the following morning. The Land Rover was constantly in four wheel drive for the trip to one of the places.

On arrival they were met by a charming elderly Scottish couple who had moved from Mombasa several years ago when she was diagnosed with respiratory problem, which was badly affected by the humidity and the coastal heat. The cooler weather and the fresh mountain air had greatly improved her health and after spending a couple of years in the mountain, she was totally cured and enjoying a happy and healthy life. She had taken up painting and had become a good artist, judging by her paintings that were displayed around the living room wall bearing her signatures. Her husband was in the process of writing a book about their life. Neither of them were of any help to Gary.

Gary was hoping that his father may have gone somewhere like that, but still could not understand the secrecy and silence behind his disappearance.

The other two places were easy to find, both places were occupied by men who had lost their partners and taken up with black mistresses. Although very courteous and friendly, these men for personal reasons were not prepared to tell their life story to a total stranger.

Four days spent in the Taita hills had failed to reveal any new leads but they had only covered one small section of this vast area.

Being a clear day without excessive cloud and fog coverage made their descent less arduous. Their progress was hampered only by the occasional forced stops to allow the brakes of their vehicle to cool down from heat generated through constant applications that caused the fluid to boil creating evaporation in the brake cylinder. However, two hours later they had safely reached the base of the mountain.

On their way through they decided to make another call at the sisal estate to see if any other information had surfaced. But neither the man they had spoken to nor his friends that he had spoken with lately had seen or heard from Gary's father.

Leaving the estate, they were held up by one of the locomotives hauling well over fifty wagons loaded with sisal leaves heading to the factory of the sixty four thousand acre property, which operated twenty four hours a day. It was owned through inheritance by the wife of a script writer residing in London, Gary was told.

From a telephone box at Voi he called Karen at her office to give her an update and advise her that after restocking his provisions and fuel, he would be targeting the other two areas of the region where he had information that many more white farming families were residing.

"Are you sure you need to do that?" she asked.

He thought he detected anxiety in her voice.

"What's the matter?" he asked.

"I have some bad news," she replied.

He hesitated for a moment, thinking that it was about his father. "What bad news?"

"Obviously you haven't read today's paper," she said.

"I haven't had the chance to read any paper for the past week. What's the bad news?"

"It is about Anthony. His wife and daughter have been kidnapped, while holidaying at a resort in Malindi, by a terrorist group from Somalia who calls themselves *'Shiftas.'* Several people were killed in the attack."

Gary was silent for a long while, and then said, "I'll drive down straight away."

After ending the phone call, they drove on and stopped at the general store and Gary bought a paper then asked Asmani to drive while he read through it.

The headline read,

"Public Servant's Wife and Daughter kidnapped in Malindi," and followed in smaller print,

"*A Public service man's wife and daughter have been kidnapped while holidaying in Malindi. The group is believed to be a terrorist group known as Shiftas based in Somalia and operating on the*

Kenyan coast province border. In an attempted robbery late yesterday, the group, which was surrounded by police, kidnapped the mother and daughter as they returned to the resort from a nearby beach, and used them as hostages for their getaway. Four resort security workers and two terrorist were killed in the process, and several people injured, the authorities are still trying to locate the hostages."

On the way down, Asmani related to Gary all he knew about the Shiftas, the exact location where one of their camps was situated near Malindi and where he suspected the hostages could be kept, due to its well protected location and the way they ran their operation. He also suspected that the hostages would be kept alive and used as a bargaining tool and could be killed if any attempt were made to free them. He told Gary that they should head directly to Malindi and check out the camp in question.

Gary agreed, but wanted to stop and see Karen first.

It was late at night, by the time they pulled in at Karen's place. Gary was badly in need of a shower and shave. He hurried in before being confronted by Denise, and asked whether he would like a shower.

After dinner he told Karen about the conversation he had with Asmani, stating that those Shiftas were brutal killers.

"They are," Karen replied. "Worse than the Mau Mau, who are actually fighting for a cause, but the Shiftas are known thieves and murderers."

She asked her house boy to organise Asmani's lodging for the night and told Gary that he should get a good night's sleep and resume his journey in the morning, and being exhausted, he totally agreed.

On several occasions he attempted to contact Anthony that evening, but without success and eventually he left him a message saying that he was on his way.

In was near midnight when Anthony finally called. Karen answered and called Gary to the phone. Anthony sounded shattered. He updated Gary on all the latest developments and Gary heard from the tension in his voice that the news was far from good.

He and Asmani left early the following morning. They made the seventy three mile journey within two hours and pulled up at the resort while breakfast was being served. Anthony was sitting at a table near the entrance in discussion with some of his officers. He spotted Gary's Land Rover, stood up and called him over and ordered him a coffee.

Chapter 25

Anthony's bloodshot eyes showed that he had not slept for several days. Concerned about his mental state, Gary asked the doctor standing nearby to follow him out of the room and enquired about Anthony's health. The doctor assured him that under the circumstances Anthony was managing fairly well, but acknowledged that he needed sleep. Gary thanked him and went back inside.

"How are you holding up?" he asked Anthony.

Trying to show strength in front of his staff, Anthony shook his head, and said he was fine.

"Do you have any plans?" Gary asked,

"Nothing specific. It's a difficult one. Using too much force could prove fatal to the girls."

"Has any contact been made?" Gary asked.

"No, that's what I am afraid of. If there is a demand, at least I could negotiate and know they are alive, but so far nothing."

Gary related the conversation he had with Asmani on the way down, and suggested that it would be important that Asmani should talk to Intelligence, to which Anthony agreed.

Asmani's interview lasted well over an hour. His information did not all coincide with that held by Intelligence, especially the track leading to the southern side of the river and the location of the camp. Furthermore, the security people were concerned about how well informed he was.

Asmani explained to them that as a kid, he frequently camped in that area with his uncle who was a poacher and he told them about the time they had to hide in a tree for hours when they came across a group of Shiftas having a disagreement and witnessed them executing their own people.

Gary was later called in, and was asked if he had any doubts over Asmani's loyalty. He assured them that Asmani had been by his side for the last six month and had found him to be very loyal. Being fluent in Somali, he then offered to go in disguised as a poacher with the off chance of finding out if the hostages were being held at that camp.

Intelligence needed to confer before making a final decision and putting a plan in place could take a couple of days. The delay was frustrating for both Gary and Asmani.

Gary told Anthony that while Intelligence were making their decision he would accompany Asmani to a place that overlooked a Shifta camp site, and hopefully return with some valuable information.

Anthony sounded very concerned for Gary's safety. "How much do you trust Asmani?" he asked.

"He has never given me doubts about his loyalty," Gary answered.

"Intelligence seems a little concerned with his statement," Anthony said.

"Right now, your wife and daughter need help and I am prepared to take that chance," Gary told him.

Reluctantly, Anthony agreed.

With Asmani driving, they left early the next day and drove north across the Tana River and continued for another fifty miles. Past the village of Msanga, they turned left on to a dirt track just before the bridge and came to a sudden stop at the water's edge where the estuary branched out into several tributaries.

"What happens here?" Gary asked.

"We have to wait for low tide to get across," Asmani replied.

"And how long will that take?"

"Two hours at the most."

Asmani explained that the only possible way of reaching their destination was either on foot by following the inlet to the river mouth twenty five miles away, which could take a couple of days, or the way they were about to attempt, by waiting for low tide and running their four wheel drive along the firm ground on the water's edge for about thirty metres or so, and then on to the track on the other side.

Gary decided that they should walk across first, and make sure that it was still passable. He took his shoes off and attempted to walk across. They waded knee deep along the water's edge and finally across to the track on the other side, which proved that Asmani's theory was right, provided that they could get their vehicle across without it sinking deep into the mud.

"The only other option," said Asmani, "is another crossing with a bridge twenty miles north, but that would take us north of the river and directly into the Shifta's camp, a stronghold that's well guarded."

They patiently waited till the tide was out then Asmani walked ahead on foot and guided Gary driving over the firm part of the crossing on the water's edge. Once they reached the track they continued on firmer ground, passing through mangroves, along swamps and coconut trees, did several turns close to other sea inlets and finally came to an open Savannah grass plain where they encountered herds of antelopes that quickly dispersed as the Land Rover went over spinifexes brushing under the carriage creating loud, scrapping, amplified noises.

They made a sharp right hand turn that took them towards the North West. After having driven for another hour or so, Asmani stopped the car on a slight ridge to get his bearing. Satisfied that he was on the right track, they continued on.

He pointed out to Gary a mountain range in the far distance, telling him that it was the place they were heading for. Another hour had passed by the time they reached the destination and to avoid being detected they would continue the rest of their journey on foot.

Chapter 26

Meanwhile, back in Malindi the police had informed Intelligence that the information Asmani had given then about a track leading to the southern side of the river was false. They produced a map that showed the water inlet ran the entire length of the road, making it impossible to cross without a bridge. In his interview, Asmani must have missed telling them that the place was only passable at low tide.

The police inspector was a bit concerned when Anthony told them that Gary and Asmani had gone ahead to survey the area and would be returning the following day and he suggested that nothing be done until they returned. The inspector wanted to call Lamu police to apprehend Gary's vehicle but Anthony talked him against doing it.

Asmani parked the Land Rover in a spot near a rocky outcrop hidden by two great boulders that seemed to have been dislodged from the hill above through erosion many years ago, rolled down the side and come to rest in the position they stood now, somehow creating a perfect hiding spot for their vehicle.

In their back packs were binoculars, water bottles, a can of corned beef, baked beans, and a torch. Armed with a rifle and a hand gun each, they set out for the seven mile walk to the supposed lookout. Once there, two hours later, they settled in a position where with the sun at their backs and using their binoculars, they had an uninterrupted view of the plains below and across the river to where Asmani had correctly stated, a few huts stood, protected from the east and north by the two hills and the river from the south which made their hide out impenetrable. Asmani confirmed that it was the Shifta camp, and although not detecting any movements around the place, he was reasonably certain that they would have their men stationed at several observation points on both hills and others guarding the entrance. They would not have bothered placing a man on the southern side as the only passable place across the river was the crossing next to their camp that would be seen from the hills and could only be accessed on foot during the dry season.

Twice, theShiftas had been attacked by police coming in from the north east side and both times they were warned by their scouts placed in the hills at the entrance. When the police arrived, they found the place deserted as they had all dispersed into the surrounding hills.

Gary and Asmani kept watch on the place and intended to keep watching till dark in the hope of seeing Anthony's wife and daughter, maybe going to the toilet or to the river for a wash.

They had been watching for a while when suddenly the figure of a white man dressed in oversized, mud-stained clothing appeared from the bush and headed across the river to the water hole near the Shifta camp. Gary nudged Asmani so hard in an attempt to point out the man, that he almost sent him tumbling down the side of a rock ledge.

Asmani looked through his binoculars, shook his head and muttered, "He cannot still be alive."

"Who is still alive?" Gary asked.

"That man is not a white man," Asmani said. "His mother and father are both black, he was born white, with funny skin, he doesn't talk, he is bad medicine, and no one would ever challenge him. There are stories going around, that if he catches you staring directly at him would put a curse on you and could kill you. Even lions and leopards will avoid attacking him."

"Sounds weird," said Gary, not believing what he had heard. "He must be an albino."

"He looks about your age," Asmani said, "but he is known to have been around forever."

Gary watched as the albino walked freely around the place unchallenged.

"He is known to walk long distances between Malindi, Kilifi, and Lamu as he travels around," Asmani continued. "People give him food and clothing. He has to keep his body covered to protect himself from the sun, so he either walks around at night, early morning or late evening."

Gary reflected for a moment, and then asked, "Do you believe all that?"

"I don't, Bwana Gazi, but I don't want to find out by being dead."

Although being attacked by tsetse flies, a fly that resembles a common house fly but bigger, flatter and tougher to kill, also known to carry sleeping sickness, Gary could not help but laugh, not for what Asmani had said, but how he said it.

It was getting dark when they attempted their journey back to the car. Wanting to travel light, they had only brought one torch but had forgotten to renew the batteries in it, leaving them with a very dim torch. Realising that it could be risky travelling in the dark, they opted to spend the night at the lookout and return early the following morning. Being full moon, they would have an excellent view of the area. The lookout being high up gave them excellent protection from some predators, but also turned out be the baboon's dormitory.

Asmani assured Gary that baboons were harmless in the dark and would not move the entire night. The downside to it was that baboons were leopard's favourite food. Being nocturnal, leopards hunt during the night. With no other option at hand, they decided to take shifts in sleeping. They were also thankful that the tsetse flies had swapped shifts with mosquitoes whose stings were less painful. They took turns in getting four hours sleep each.

At dawn, they noticed smoke coming from the huts, they kept close watch on the camp through their binoculars and along the river's edge bordering the camp. A couple of native women were at the water's edge, filling up their water buckets and carrying them balanced on their heads back to camp. Gary kept his binoculars affixed on them while Asmani concentrated on the surrounding areas with his.

As the two women reached the camp, a white woman appeared from out of the hut. It could be Anthony's wife

Gary whispered to himself, he could not be certain from that distance. and there was no sign of the daughter.

With that knowledge on hand, they quickly made their way back to the Land Rover, hoping that Intelligence hadn't gone into action before their return. With the tide still a fair way up on arrival at the crossing, they were forced to wait for several hours. Walking along the edge of a river that was full of fish, Gary wished that he had carried a fishing line in his Land Rover as he could have passed the time doing a spot of fishing while waiting for the tide to subside. He also spotted crabs and the odd lobster feeding along the deeper part of the water's edge. Obviously crustaceans were abundant in these parts and were definitely not on the natives' specialty list.

They pulled in at the resort car park at exactly 3.30pm. Anthony was frantically pacing up and down the footpath in front of the resort pool, obviously relieved when he spotted Gary's Land Rover driving in and he rushed over to meet him.

He was delighted with the information Gary had brought back and with the description and of the type of clothes she was wearing, with no other white women declared missing in Kenya at the time, Anthony was confident that it was his wife. As for his daughter, he confirmed that she was always a late riser.

Anthony called an urgent meeting with Intelligence, and the local police inspector. Gary was invited to give the information he had. He described his trip, how they had got across the river and what he had discovered. The others all sat there looking dumbfounded.

Together with the police inspector and Intelligence they were asked to put forward a plan.

Gary's plan was to have Kelelu, his right hand man from the KPR join him on this project, set up a base camp at the turn-off, hidden from the main highway and remove the Albino from the scene by capturing him and holding him at the base. Then they would find someone with skills in disguise who could make Gary look like the albino with enough facial covering, obtain a pair of sandals made from old tyres, and give him a quick lesson on handling a bow and arrow.

With that in place, Gary and his men would try to infiltrate the kidnapper's camp by posing as poachers, and the albino with a team of Malindi Police close by as back up.

Apart from apprehending the albino, everything else was put in place and Kelelu was booked on the next flight in. Apprehending the albino was a problem as he was not easy to locate and the attempt could alert the kidnappers.

The entire operation would be run by the police inspector who possessed local knowledge, closely guided by Intelligence.

The base would be manned by two white police officers and seven Askaries. Another armed unit consisting of two white officers and eight Askaries would be sent to the next entry, near the town of Lamu in an attempt to stop anyone from entering or leaving the area. Radio contact would be set to both bases and field personnel.

Chapter 27

A day later, all was in place on low tide from the base camp at the turn off. Gary, Asmani and Kelelu set out in their Land Rover, followed in another by a white police officer, three Askaries and a tracker. They continued to the spot near the boulders where the two Land Rovers were left, guarded by an Askari.

They walked the seven miles to the lookout where the officer and his Askaries would stay to monitor the operation, and keep contact with base.

They spent the rest of the day observing the area and not once spotting the albino. After conferring with Intelligence and the police officer, Gary decided to put his plan in motion. Being full moon, they would wait till it rose which would give them enough light without using a torch to navigate their way to their side of the river, and stay far enough away to avoid being trampled by the hippos that roam on land to graze during the night.

Disguised as the albino, Gary went ahead, keeping a close watch on the surroundings in case he was spotted and able to alert Kelelu and Asmani who were following him a short distant away, fully armed and dressed like poachers, carrying minimal amounts of provisions with them to the bank of the river on the southern side.

From the lookout, radio contact would only be maintained to warn of the kidnapper's position or the albino's sighting.

Reaching their destination around midnight, they settled quietly on a flat area well protected by trees and shrubs. The silence was suddenly broken by Asmani letting out a muffled yell. Gary and Kelelu turned towards him and saw that a huge python had wrapped itself around his body in an attempt to squeeze the breath out of him. Kelelu quickly pulled out his knife grabbed the giant snake by the head and set out to try and cut its neck off, while Gary kept pulling the tail away from Asmani's body. As swiftly as it had appeared, the giant snake let go and slipped away in the dark towards the river bank. It took Asmani several minutes to regain his composure while Kelelu could not stop laughing, saying that the snake's release of Asmani was because he was too skinny and smelly. On recovering their composure, they sat and waited for dawn when they would move closer to the river bank into a hiding position.

Gary with a hand gun lodged on his right butt under his makeshift pair of pants secured by a piece of rope that was also holding up his pants, had started his walk towards the shallow part of the river in an attempt to get across at the point where he had seen the albino crossing a couple of days earlier. His tyre sandals had malfunctioned and were hurting as he was displaying a slight limp that somehow suited the image.

The two women fetching water made a sudden retreat as he was spotted. Gary wandered over and sat on a rock pretending to be washing his sore foot, at the same time surveying the huts. The previous routine was repeated, but this time, the older white women and a younger one appeared at the same time and Gary identified them as Anthony's wife and daughter. They had fence wiring wrapped tightly around their wrists and they were tied together by a two metre length of rope.

He did not detect any other movement around and decided to move closer and investigate. As he got up from the rock he was sitting on, the two women were forced back into the hut. Gary walked towards the back of the huts and cast his eyes towards the hill. As expected, he spotted two men on the ridge watching the eastern entrance, but they were avoiding eye contact with him.

He kept moving around till he reached the front of the hut where one of the woman brought out a badly battered tin plate on which were two pieces of cassava, a cob of corn and a piece of salted dried fish. She placed the plate on a rock ledge a few metres away, gesturing that it was for him and left, without making eye contact with him.

He was not sure how to handle the food, but instinct told him to pick it up and put it in his pocket, which he did, and lowered his head in a thank you gesture, took a few steps away and sat on a rock pretending to eat. The corn was quite palatable, but he did not give the fish a try.

He sat there for another half hour and during that time saw no signs of any male around. Still displaying a limp, he moved across towards the river bank where he made the crossing earlier, continually watching for any activities from within the camp, until he finally reached his men. They conferred and decided to make their move. Gary radioed the officer at the lookout that he was ready to invade the camp. The officer responded that he had been closely monitoring his move through the binoculars, and had already dispatched his Askaries and tracker and would only be minutes away.

The plan to free the hostages was put in motion.

Anthony was waiting at the base camp that was set near the turn-off when the news reached him that both his wife and daughter had been sighted and the operation to free them was in progress.

Asmani was sent to approach the camp from the western side, armed and dressed as a poacher. Being fluent in Somali, he would strike up a conversation with the two women. Gary crossed the river again and sat on the rock in the shade at the river's edge, where he could clearly see both Asmani and Kelelu and waited for Kelelu's signal to let him know when backup had arrived.

Asmani established that the abductors' leader and a few of his men were in town, leaving the two women and the three men guarding the hostages. Instead of one of the women taking food to the men guarding the entrance from the hill, the man offered to go instead, leaving the place unprotected, so they thought.

With the plan in motion, Kelelu gave Gary the all clear sign. In turn Gary passed it on to Asmani who drew his gun on the two women. Like wild beasts they both lunged at him, yelling at the top of their voices loud enough to be heard by the men up on the hill. Their combined strength had him on the ground, kicking and attempting to choke him. Seeing that Asmani was in trouble Gary went to his aid. Petrified at seeing the albino, the women let go of his throat, giving Asmani time to unsheathe his razor sharp dagger and slash their throats. Gary stood motionless for a while, trying to digest the scene that confronted him.

The yelling must have echoed through the valley. Gary looked up the hill to where the three male abductors were but could not see them. They had obviously heard the yell and were on their way in. He figured that it would take them at least ten minutes to get back, giving him ample time to get the hostages away, even if they had to be carried.

Inside the hut in a dark corner at the back, Anthony's wife and daughter sat crouched and holding on to each other. Their fright increased as they were confronted by the dirty white person walking towards them and his voice calling out to them that he was Gary was not recognised.

After a long silence and reflection, and in a soft voice, Jessica asked, "Is it really you Gary?"

"Yes it is."

"Why are you dressed like that?" she asked, sobbing.

He grinned and said, "It's a long story, I'll tell you later."

Not able to undo their metal ties he cut the rope and asked them to follow him closely.

Kelelu and his Askaries had crossed the river, giving Gary and the hostages cover as they attempted the river crossing on their walk to safety. They had just managed to get across the river, when they heard gun fire, and took shelter in the long grassy area next to a clump of trees and waited until all was quiet.

The walk back to the lookout was long and tedious. A Landover had been dispatched to proceed as far as possible to pick up the hostages but could only get within four miles past the lookout, leaving them a walk of three miles, which they managed to complete in just over an hour.

Within two hours, Anthony had arrived at the meeting place at the boulders, accompanied by a doctor in a long wheel base Land Rover, fitted out as an ambulance. Tears of joy appeared as he was reunited with his family.

Asmani's throat was checked by the doctor; apart from being extremely swollen and badly bruised, he was told that he would survive.

Kelelu, the white officer and his Askaries fatally wounded one of the abductors and captured two more as they came running down from the hill with their guns blazing. With more police Askaries arriving as back up, two were sent to take the abductors' position on the hill to set an ambush and wait for the others to turn up.

It was fairly late in the afternoon when two vehicles drove in with five men in one and three in the other. They alighted from their vehicles with bottles of alcohol in their hands while still consuming the contents. Either seeing that their men was on the hills and unaware that anything was wrong or plainly too drunk to care, they casually started walking towards the huts, carrying a couple of bottles of beer for the two women, and yelling for them to come out. The police fired over their heads from their ambush position and told them to drop to the ground. Their leader who went for his hand gun was shot in the chest and the rest of them quickly surrendered and were taken into custody. On their side, one of the police Askari had a gunshot wound in the leg, the others including Gary came through the ordeal with only minor cuts, scratches and badly stung by tsetse flies.

The bodies were removed, and as was the practice the camp was searched and torched.

Chapter 28

Anthony and his family were rushed back to Malindi, where a plane was waiting to fly them to Nairobi.

Gary, Kelelu and Asmani decided to spend the night at the base camp. Gary had a swim in the salt water of the estuary and tried to clean as much make up as possible off him without the use of soap and then changed clothes from his albino attire back to his normal wear.

As soon as it got dark with the incoming tide, they set out looking for crabs at the water's edge of the inlet; they returned an hour later with a bucket full of crays and mud crabs. They unearthed a half-cut ten gallon metal drum found buried at the water's edge, filled it up with salt water, lit a fire, cooked and feasted on their catch.

Unshaven, unwashed for close to four days, Gary's appearance reminded him of the old man he had met in the Taita hills as he looked in the rear vision mirror on his way to Malindi the following morning. He called in at the central police station to report, as per the request of the inspector who was running the operation. Once there, he would take the opportunity to use their phone to call Karen.

He noticed a smirk on the inspector's face as he entered his office, with a smidgen of make-up still plastered all over the exposed parts of his body. He realised that it would cause anyone to take a second look. Standing and waiting for the inspector to ask why he wanted to see him, he heard the door open and a familiar voice, saying, "Do you think you need a shower, dear?"

He could not mistake the voice of Karen's mother. He turned around and there was Denise with Karen who had just arrived from Mombasa to meet him. The strong smell of crabs and lobsters that he had eaten the night before didn't deter her from giving him a loving hug and a kiss while tears freely flowed from both eyes down her cheeks.

Holding him tightly, she whispered, "You are an incredible person, is there a limit to your talent?"

After releasing him, Karen told him that Intelligence wanted him to fly to Nairobi as soon as possible for a debriefing and she had been asked to accompany him.

The Askaries who had taken part in the rescue were at the station busily exchanging tales with Asmani and Kelelu about their encounters. The inspector assured Gary that both his men would be well rewarded for their efforts. Asmani was offered a post with the Malindi Police and knowing that he had committed himself to helping Gary, the position would be left open until he was ready.

Gary was badly in need of a shower, and decided to use the shower room at the station. He spent a long time trying to remove all the makeup that had been applied over his body but realised that he would need a hot shower to achieve a better result and would have to wait till he reached Karen's place in Mombasa.

The three of them followed Karen back to her house, Asmani and Kelelu were accommodated in the houseboy dwelling. Gary stopped at the front door, and called out, "I am going to have a shower," much to the amusement of Denise and Karen.

Although he finally looked and felt clean and shaved, he appeared for dinner looking very tired. For dinner, the houseboy had prepared a leg of lamb, made some incisions in the meat and inserted bacon, garlic, and other spices and it was cooked to perfection, accompanied by baked potatoes, carrots, sweet potatoes, pumpkins, freshly picked green beans and a mint sauce. Gary managed two servings.

The phone rang around 8.00pm; it was Anthony wanting to speak to Gary, and after a moment of silence that felt like an eternity, he thanked Gary for his help and apologised for leaving before his return. Again saying how grateful he was and telling him that both his wife and daughter were fine, he insisted that Gary come up to Nairobi as soon as possible. He sounded like his old self again and Gary assured him he would get the first available flight. He hung up the phone, reflected for a moment then asked Karen if she could get reservations on the first available flight.

"We already have an open ticket," she replied. "The planes are never fully booked; we could leave tomorrow if you are up to it."

After dinner they sat on the veranda looking at the moon. Vision of the previous day's event kept haunting him and although he realised that there were no other options, he still kept trying to justify the events in his mind. Karen must have noticed the pensive mood he was displaying and kept by his side the whole evening until she went to call Anthony to confirm that they would be on the next day's flight. On her return, she found him asleep in the easy chair. Not wanting to disturb him, she put a light blanket over him while she sat there and watched him sleep.

Kelelu had been given a week's leave and decided to explore Mombasa with Asmani. He asked Karen if he could stay for a few more days. She told them both that they were welcome to stay for as long as they wanted and told her house boy to make sure that they were well fed and looked after.

Chapter 29

Their flight to Nairobi the following day would take over an hour. Never having been on a plane before, Gary was both apprehensive and excited, although he tried hard not to show it.

On boarding the plane, knowing the great aerial view that they would encounter passing near the Kilimanjaro on the flight to Nairobi, Karen insisted that he should have the window seat. Gary being the gentleman refused saying that she should have it. Eventually Karen had to lie and tell him that she preferred the aisle seat as she could take a walk to stretch her legs during the trip.

She detected a slight nervousness in him as the plane accelerated to get airborne. Both his hands were tightly clutching on to his arm rests and in fact, he was gripping them so hard that blood had stopped circulation to his fingers which were slowly turning blue. She tried to distract his attention by engaging in a conversation, but he did not respond. Eventually, with great difficulty, she managed to prise his hands away from the arm rests, pretending that she was nervous and needed to hold on to his hand.

When the plane finally reached its cruising height he settled a little and enjoyed the view from his window seat. But the sudden air pocket they encountered north of Kilimanjaro definitely did not help matters. It was one of the worst, the pilot later told them, apparently a drop of over a hundred feet. Gary had finally relaxed enough to get his speech back when the pilot announced their descent into Nairobi airport and the nerves took control again.

Very unlike him, Karen thought, *to show that he was not in control.*

Back on solid ground, he soon regained his composure and like a little boy, started describing how quick the trip was and how he enjoyed the view. Somehow did not mention the air pocket.

They were met at the airport by an officer from Intelligence and were taken to their hotel rooms next to one another organised by either Anthony or his department.

Within the hour, just after they had got settled, Anthony arrived to pick them up. He put his arms around Gary, held him silently for a good minute, and in a sombre voice, said, "Fate must have brought us together. Despite all the resources at my disposal, my wife and daughter may not have been alive today without your help. I will never be able to do enough to thank you and your men for what you have done putting your lives at risk."

Gary shrugged it off, saying, "You would have done the same for me."

"You are both my special guests," said Anthony. "And tonight we will celebrate my good fortune. I will have the honour of introducing you both to my friends."

Karen decided to stay back and rest as Anthony took Gary to Intelligence headquarters for debriefing. On arrival, Gary was shown to a room where two officers from Intelligence and a psychologist sat waiting for him.

The debriefing consisted of nothing but questions about what actually happened, how did he come to the decision to take the course of action he took, and why. What made him believe that the information he received from Asmani was reliable enough to ignore advice from Malindi Police? When that was over, Gary was criticised heavily for not following orders. The whole debacle went for over an hour.

After the debriefing, they explained to Gary the reason for having the psychologist present was to help Anthony's wife Jessica to openly talk about her ordeal, which would help towards her recovery.

After the debriefing was complete, Jessica entered and came over and kissed Gary on the cheek and gave his arm a gentle squeeze. She looked tired and withdrawn. They moved to the next room where a dozen or so lounge chairs were placed in a semi-circle around a low table. After some pleasantries were exchanged, the two officers excused themselves and left, leaving them at the mercy of the psychologist.

Jessica was asked to describe her ordeal as best she could remember. Hesitantly, with considerable stress in her voice, she began.

"We were returning from the beach by using the entrance that leads to the basement of the resort. As we reached the entry door we heard shots. We were hesitant at first to go in, but soon dismissed it thinking the group of children we recently saw playing outside were letting off fire crackers.

"As we reached the top of the stairs, just before the entrance to the foyer, a man appeared, grabbed me and put a knife to my throat. Another man came from behind and grabbed Corinne. They dragged us inside the foyer, tied our hands behind our back and blindfolded us. There was a lot of loud shouting in the Somali language and the gun fire ceased. We were dragged to a waiting car somewhere close by and driven out of town. One of our abductors who spoke English told us that if we did not want to be harmed we had to obey his orders.

"It felt that we had been driving for an hour and then had a change of vehicle and driven for another hour before we came to a stop. We were dragged out and made to walk in the hot sun for well over an hour to our destination where we were given a drink of water. Our hands were untied from behind our backs, and then retied on our front by a wire band permanently tied around our wrist with some sort of tools. At night we were kept tied together by a length of rope that was also secured to our wrist bands.

"The blindfolds were eventually removed by one of the women attending to us. There were lots of male voices on the first day of our arrival but by the second day after spotting a white albino man who appeared from nowhere, most of them vanished.

"The floor in the hut was plain, hardened, red dirt, some straw was stacked in the corner of the room and we used this as bedding. Through the gaps we could see people moving about outside. We spent the entire night constantly being bitten by mosquitoes and other bugs, and the occasional noises from wild animals scavenging around the camp made it impossible to get any sleep.

"We were given one meal a day which consisted of corn, sweet potatoes dried beans and a piece of dried fish, which we were supposed to only smell while we ate the crushed corn. The smell of the dried fish was enough to put us off eating anything, there were no toilet facilities so we ate and drank as little as possible to avoid going to the toilet.

"On the following night the two women who shared our hut gathered some firewood and lit a fire in the fire pit in the centre of the hut. Even though it created a lot of smoke causing us to have coughing fits and difficulty in breathing, somehow it helped disperse the mosquitoes.

"We were petrified that night, as several men took turns appearing like ghosts through the doorway and went over to where the younger woman was sleeping. We would hear rumbles through the hay, heavy breathing and once the deed was done they would leave, and not long after another would appear. We were so scared every time someone entered, that we limited our breathing and did not move a muscle.

"We were not allowed to the river to wash, one of the women would fetch a bucket of water, which we would drink and wash from in the hut."

The psychologist sat there motionless, absorbing and taking notes, every now and then and encouraged her to continue as if he was totally enjoying the story.

"After the second day I seemed to have lost count of how many days we had been held captive. One evening, the abductor who spoke English and seemed to be their leader arrived and took Corrine away with him. I was petrified and started yelling at him, the women tried to hold me down but I fought back. They eventually subdued me and put a dirty cloth in my mouth, my body was bruised and scratched from kicking, the older women received a deep gash on her face.

"The man returned a little while later, slapped me across the face and put a knife at my throat.

"Where did you take my daughter?" I screamed at him.

"He assured me that she was okay, and told me to shut up. After I had calmed down, he started questioning me.

"What were you doing in Malindi?" he asked.

"I was having a holiday with my daughter," I replied.

"What does your husband do?" he asked.

"He's a public servant in Nairobi," I said.

"Write down your address and your contact number," he ordered and I did.

"He studied it carefully then left and returned soon after with Corrine, I held her and made sure she had not been harmed. Apparently he had separated us to make sure the information we gave matched, as he had asked Corrine similar questions, and her answers corresponded with mine. Then he left.

"Soon after, we heard movements outside and through the gap saw that they were planning to leave. Some of them had their guns on their shoulders and a bag in their hands. As one of the women came into the hut, we stopped watching and turned away from the gap. We heard voices fading as they got further away and soon the place was in silence apart from the noise of the river over the crossing nearby and the odd chirping of the birds.

"We endured the same problems with the smoke that night and apart from the two women there was only one elderly man left in the camp that we could see.

"The routine continued the following morning. Both of the women had gone to the river to fetch water and as we both went out to have a wash from the bucket, we noticed that the albino had returned. The two women looked very agitated and ushered us back inside. It was really funny that morning when the albino appeared sitting on the rock close to the huts. Corrine looked through the gap of the hut and said the albino is back, and after a moment's pause, she said he looks like Gary."

"How did you feel when Corrine was returned unharmed?" the psychologist asked.

Jessica hesitated for a second looked at Gary, as if to say, *what kind of a question is that?* Not getting a reply, she went on.

"Knowing that she hadn't been harmed felt good, although I was suffering from a sore jaw. About losing my cool, I felt a bit silly."

The psychologist gave a comforting smile. "I understand," he said. "Why don't you carry on?"

"When the commotion started that morning we heard a male voice and the two women were wrestling, yelling and fighting with a man near the hut entrance. I feared for the worst, I thought that maybe another tribe had attacked and when I heard the women's cries being muffled, I knew we would be next, so I grabbed Corrine and retreated to the darker end of the hut and held her tightly. After the two women had been silenced there was a sudden quietness that felt like an eternity before we heard someone call out that he was Gary. We dismissed it, because somehow it did not sound like the Gary we knew, but remembering what Corrine had said that the albino looked like Gary, it eventually hit home that Corinne was right, the albino was in fact Gary and we were being rescued."

"How did you react knowing that maybe you were being rescued?" the psychologist asked.

Jessica reflected for a while.

"With everything that was going on, I just felt helpless, it felt that I was being awaken from a bad dream. I felt traumatised I held on to Corrine and just followed Gary's instructions. At the same time, I was concerned that Gary was limping and I wanted to help him."

"During that whole ordeal, which part did you find most distressing?" asked the psychologist.

"When the man came and took my daughter away, and the night when the men kept appearing through the hut entrance."

Ending the session, the psychologist took over and explained to her that she had gone through a terrible ordeal that could have affected her for the rest of her life. But as she was a strong person, and being able to talk about it and with regular counselling would soon put her on the road to full recovery.

Outside, Anthony and Corrine were waiting. Jessica appeared more relaxed as she joined them. They waited till Gary was finished and drove him back to his hotel.

Chapter 30

The Tudor room at the Restaurant where Karen took Gary while in Nairobi was booked for the night by Anthony. They were picked up from their hotel and driven to the venue by security personnel.

Karen was dressed in a long evening gown that fitted perfectly around her slim body. She looked elegant and beautiful, Gary thought. Gary had hired himself a suit from the hotel hire department, and although not being used to dressing up, it fitted him perfectly and gave him a debonair look and came to the conclusion that dressing up was not all that bad.

On arrival they were met and greeted in the foyer by Anthony, Jessica and Corrine. Both girls looked a little drawn out, which had to be expected after their ordeal, but both were very elegantly dressed.

In attendance were mainly Anthony's closest friends. Also present was the Governor of Kenya, the Police Commissioner and the Army Chief. In all, there were close to forty people there.

When planning the seating, Anthony had wanted to put Gary and Karen at his table, but remembering Gary's loathing of being the centre of attention, decided against it. Instead, he put him and Karen at a table that was set for six next to his.

Gary thought he recognised two familiar faces as he entered the room, but dismissed the possibility. As he and Karen were being escorted around and introduced to Anthony's friends, his eyes kept wondering towards the room to where the familiar faces he thought he recognised were, but could no longer see them.

At the end of the introductions, they returned to their allocated table. Gary found it odd that it was set for six, and only the two of them sat at it, but decided not to worry about it. Then in came the two familiar faces he thought he had recognised earlier, dressed in their tuxedoes accompanied by their partners being ushered to their table. Gary still couldn't recognise them especially when dressed so formally.

His eyes lit up as they got closer. He was ecstatic and for a person who did not show emotion, tears of joy were freely running down his cheeks. But he quickly regained his composure and shook hands with them both.

Anthony watching from his table was relieved to see that the choice of asking the captain and Sergeant Thom was all worthwhile and totally appreciated by Gary.

The evening went well, the meals were great, they danced, Gary was enjoying the rendezvous with his old friends, and had a drink or two more than he normally would.

"He is such a good looking man and you two make a perfect couple," said a female voice from behind Karen.

Karen turned, and saw the commissioner's wife standing there.

"Hello!" Karen said, smiling.

"He looks much younger than I anticipated, to have carried such an amazing rescue," the Governor's wife said. "You make a wonderful couple."

Karen smiled again. "Thank you," she said.

They exchanged pleasantries and talked for a while. The commissioner's wife wanted to have them over for drinks the following day, but as they had made arrangement to have lunch at Anthony's place, and had to catch their flight back to Mombasa, Karen had to decline the invitation but thanked her anyway.

On the way back to their hotel, she told Gary about the conversation. "There can't be too many people who can boast about refusing an invitation to have drinks with the Governor and his wife," she said.

They both laughed.

They arrived at Anthony's place at mid-day. Karen was wearing a white pair of slacks and a blue frilly top with a white and blue checked scarf. Gary was back in his usual comfortable pair of slacks, a tee shirt and light blue jumper.

"This is more a relaxed family get together," Anthony said. "Let's have a drink!"

He took Gary to the board room, where a well-stocked bar stood in the corner.

"What's your poison?" he asked. "No, cancel that! I have to give you a man's drink!" He took two whisky glasses from the shelf and quarter filled them from a bottle at the back of the cabinet. "This is older than both of us," he said with a wide grin. "It's sixty years old. I've kept it for a special occasion, and now the day is here."

He gave Gary a glass and took his own, lifted touched Gary's glass and said, "Cheers!"

Gary took a sip and nearly stopped breathing, but recovered after a few sharp coughs. It was strong but smooth.

"One of the great peaty monsters from Islay on the west coast of Scotland," Anthony said. "My absolute favourite."

Gary took another, more cautious sip and savoured the powerful smell of peat and the wonderful, smooth way the liquor rolled on his tongue before warming a path all the way down.

"What are your plans once you have located your father?" Anthony asked.

"To go to University I hope, but for now everything is up in the air," Gary replied.

"With the information we both have, I'm sure you will soon find him."

"I hope you are right," Gary said. "By the way I must thank you for your help by allowing Karen to take time off to help me."

"That's the least I can do Gary, I owe you a great deal more than you may imagine. By the way, how serious are you and Karen?"

"We are very good friends."

"That's a shame, because I think you two are great together."

Gary felt like confiding in him about their age differences, but figured that Anthony knew that already.

"I have a proposition for you," Anthony said. "I don't want you to give me an answer now, but I want you to think about it, talk it over with Karen if you want."

"What is it?"

"I want to offer you a job with my department."

"Anthony, I don't know a thing about security," said Gary. "But the grilling I received from the police chief in Malindi and the warning I received from your department would indicate that I'm not very good at taking direct orders. Beside you've done enough to repay me for the help that I gave you."

"Don't get me wrong," Anthony said. "I'm not doing this to repay you, on the contrary my department needs someone like you. Please tell me you will at least think about it?"

Gary realised that he was serious. "I will," he said.

They went back and had their lunch, and Jessica brought out the bottle of champagne that she had saved, which they all shared. They spent the entire afternoon exchanging jokes and laughing until it was time to leave for the airport accompanied by Anthony and Jessica.

The flight back encountered less turbulence than coming up.

Chapter 31

With the Land Rover packed with their essentials, Gary and Asmani said their farewells to Kelelu at the airport as they headed off for the second part of their journey visiting the Taita Taveta district in search of Bwana Maxi. They made another stop at Voi police station to inform the Superintendent of their presence in the area, and were met by the officer who had a run in with Karen, only this time he was an entirely different person, he was friendly, well-mannered and gave Gary some useful information.

The police officer had located a man who said that he knew Bwana Maxi several years ago. He was the father of the local mechanic who had inspected the Land Rover before its purchase.

Accompanied by the police officer, Gary drove down to the local garage and had a talk to the old man. To Gary's surprise, he was assured by the old man that Bwana Maxi still owned the Sisal Plantation. He also told him about Bwana Maxi's long-time girlfriend who lived near the town of Moshi in the state of Tanganyika. He drew Gary a mud map showing the location of the property on the northern side of the town, at the base of Mount Kilimanjaro. The police officer who accompanied Gary offered to check on the ownership of the Sisal Plantation but Gary said that it would be quicker done through the Department of Internal Security. Gary thanked him for his help and left.

With another five hours of day light remaining, they set out to find the girlfriend and have a talk to her. After driving for three hours over undulating hills, creek crossings and corrugated roads, they finally arrived at where the mud map indicated the property was situated. But the location was in dense forest that had never been farmed or inhabited. Gary started having doubts about the old Indian's mental capacity. After driving around for another hour, they finally found someone who knew of the place, which happened to be on the southern side of the town and guided them there.

When they reached the small farm house and knocked on the door, a woman came and and stared at the arrivals.

"Who are you?" she demanded in unfriendly tones.

"I'm sorry to bother you," said Gary. "I was told that I might find my father here. I've been looking for him for a long time."

The hostility faded and after a few questions, the woman said that she was well acquainted with Gary's father. In fact, she even admitted that they were once a close item, but she assured Gary that she had not seen him for well over a year.

"That's nothing unusual for Max," she said. "Once, he had been gone for well over eighteen months, and then one day he drove in as if nothing had changed. I got used to him, that was Max and no one could change him. And who would want to?"

"I am really glad to have met you," said Gary.

She offered him and Asmani accommodation for the night.

"I have known your father for well over twelve years," she said. "He is very different to anyone I have ever met. He is in his own way kind, gentle and sincere. Loves his whisky and I always keep a couple of bottles of his favourite brand for when he visits, which I hope will be soon."

She prepared a delicious Irish stew for dinner, which both men enjoyed immensely. She told Gary about her coming to East Africa in her mid-twenties just before the war, employed by the British Government to do humanitarian work and when her contract expired, was given a job in the Department of Labour and Industry until she retired a few years ago at the age of forty five. She met Max when he came to her department to get a permit to recruit workers from the State of Tanganyika to work on his sisal plantation and from there their friendship grew.

The following morning, having received another confidence boost that his father could still be alive, Gary thanked her for her hospitality and promised to keep her updated on the outcome of his search, said a fond farewell and the two men left.

Two hours later they turned left into another dirt road that headed west towards another hill area of the Taita Taveta district. The climb was nowhere near as steep as the previous Taita hills they encountered from the Mwatate side, but still slow going. The track zigzagged its way up the mountain and eventually to the plateau above.

Since no police post existed in that area, they went to the village and introduced themselves to the chief and seek permission to camp on his land. Unlike the rest of the chiefs that he had come across, usually very old men, the chief here was a young man in his late twenties or early thirties. He had a vague look in his eyes, suggesting that he may have recently had a quick drag on some forbidden weeds.

Unlike other tribes in Kenya the Taita Taveta tribes have fair complexion, slim looking and possess finer features and are good looking and friendly. Their slim build, both in the male and female, is thought to result from their diet and the amount of exercise they get climbing the hills.

The chief gave them permission to camp at a vacant hut at the village next door to the football ground and told them that the tribe's yearly dance ceremony would be taking place at the football ground later that evening. Gary and Asmani would be welcome to attend and even participate if they wished. The chief also said that most of the white people residing in his district would also be attending.

Gary and Asmani made some inquiries about Bwana Maxi and Josef with the locals around the village. Several of the older men knew of Bwana Maxi from the Sisal Estate, but could not remember seeing him recently. Eventually, a young woman came forward stating that she knew a man named Josef working for a very rich master in Mombasa and he had returned to the village for a holiday while his Master was away. She offered to accompany them to his village.

Full of anticipation they partly drove as far as the

vehicle could take them and walked the rest of the way, arriving at a group of a dozen huts spread in an area of about an acre, surrounded by banana trees and rows of cassava crops planted in between. Their guide escorted them straight to Josef's hut and called out to him.

The man who came out to greet them was obviously a well paid employee. He was neatly dressed, with nicely polished leather shoes that did not look like hand-me-downs from his master, his hut where his parents resided looked to be well maintained with nice wooden flooring and modestly furnished.

Gary introduced himself and explained the purpose of his visit. Joseph seemed happy to talk but after a short conversation, they realised that they had the wrong man. This Joseph, with a differently spelled name, worked for a Bwana Bennett in Mombasa, who at the moment was overseas and that this Joseph had not heard of a Bwana Maxi.

Again, after another failed lead they returned to the village camp, thanked the young women for her time and gave her a couple of shillings. She seemed a little hesitant in accepting such a lot of money, but Gary assured her that it was fine, hoping that she would spread the news around and might help bring forward someone with valid information.

The dance ceremony was extremely colourful and attracted a large crowd, including many white people as the chief had earlier indicated. It started with energetic men dancers, who in similarity style to the Maasai, jumped up and down in one spot in an attempt to reach the greatest height.

Gary was amazed of how fit these people were, able to continue at the pace they were setting for such long periods.

The tribal dance on the other hand was somehow very different. It was an erotic dance involving both sexes. It reminded him of the Sega dance, that the natives from his home in the Seychelles performed. The dance increased in tempo as the night went on and the local brew known as *Mbangara*, was freely being passed around and consumed by all.

The Taita Taveta tribe must be a peaceful tribe, Gary thought. Despite the amount of alcohol drunk that night, not once did a disagreement occur. The drunks were peacefully sleeping it off, while others kept the party going.

A couple of journalists from an overseas magazine who was there to witness and report on the ceremony, had parked their vehicle next to Gary's and intended to sleep in it during the night. They came over and introduced themselves and asked if he did not mind them parking next to him. He assured them that it was fine by him.

During the evening, they were interviewing a young native man who told them that he had recently got married. When asked why he did not bring his wife to the dance, he replied that he did and pointed to a young girl being fondled by another man. When the journalist asked whether he was disturbed by what was taking place, he gave him a bewildered look and dismissed it with a laugh, then went on to say, "If he is silly enough to have sex with her it will be his loss, because if he produces a child, I gain, because if it is a girl, I get the dowry when she takes a husband, and if it is a boy I get a helper."

Gary was having trouble understanding the reasoning, but agreed that it made a sort of sense.

Gary saw the similarity to the way of the Maasai tribesmen, who follow and protect their cattle while grazing. On their travels, if they came across another of their tribesmen's huts, they would leave their spears outside and spend the night with the wife. Should the husband return and find the spears, he would not enter the hut until the tribesman departed.

The music consisted mainly of bongo type drums that kept thumping out the same beat throughout the night, sending the dancers into a hypnotic state. By midnight, there were more people passed out on the ground than those standing, mostly from excessive consumption of the brew than exhaustion. The witchdoctor who made his appearance dressed in his colourful head gear with a couple of bird of paradise feathers stuck in the side, was totally ignored by half of his subjects who were either too intoxicated or exhausted, to take any notice of him.

Apart from a few dogs seen scavenging around for scraps left by the party goers, and a few vultures circling above, with their eyes fixed on the motionless bodies lying about on the ground below, the place was totally deserted the following morning. Even Asmani, his trusted offsider had not yet surfaced, and Gary had no idea where he had disappeared to.

He drove out to visit a property that he passed a few miles from the village on his way in the day before to make some enquiries. As he turned into its driveway, he came across an elderly man driving a tractor that was pulling a massive tree branch behind it.

He stopped, and came over, asking if Gary was lost and needed some help. He turned out to be a friendly person.

"You may be wondering why I am towing such a large tree branch behind a tractor," he told Gary. "As we do not have a grader at our disposal, it is another way of filling those potholes created by the recent heavy rain. It may not do as good a job as a grader but it sure helps.

He turned out to be a person who had vast knowledge and qualifications on farming in Africa, and was at the moment doing a trial on growing and supplying chilli to the East African market. He already had ten acres of various chillies under cultivation, and was in the process of setting up a factory. He was however, having difficulty getting labour to harvest his crop as the natives were not accustomed to the heat chillies generated and affected their eyes when not handled with care. During their conversation he told Gary that he knew of his father, although never had the chance to meet him.

On his way back to the village Gary picked up a dozen eggs and made himself an omelette for lunch which he shared with the two journalists who had just surfaced from their tent.

By late that afternoon a few groans were heard from the nearby bushes as the party revellers recovering from their ordeals started to appear. Asmani somehow was still nowhere to be seen. It was hours later that he eventually made a sheepish appearance. Looking at his condition Gary was contemplating taking him to hospital if there was one nearby, but he brightened up a little, after being given a cup of black coffee.

Gary came to the conclusion that this event only happens once a year because it takes them a whole year to recover.

Chapter 32

Two days since the celebration and the place was still extremely quiet compared to the day they arrived. During the hour it took them to make their descent and reach the village at the base, they only encountered a handful of people. It seemed that the whole tribe must have attended the ceremony.

From the base of the Taita Taveta Hills, they headed straight for the sisal plantation in which his father once had a half share, to talk to the owner. The plantation was a much smaller holding than the one they had previously visited, consisting of only twelve thousand acres. The transport system was not as elaborate either. It did not possess a rail system and the sisal leaves were carted by tractors towing two trailers at a time.

The small office was situated next to the factory. Gary entered the reception and asked to see the manager. The woman at the reception gave him a blank look as if she had seen a ghost, but managed a smile. She excused herself and went to get the manager.

Gary heard a few words being exchanged in the background, but could not make out what was said. She soon returned, accompanied by a man who greeted him with an accent that he had not heard before and could not identify. The man also gave Gary a strange look as he made his appearance and said he was Francis Gerard, the estate manager.

Gary introduced himself, and explained the reason for his visit. There was a sudden silence. One could have heard a pin drop.

Gerard apologised for his surprised behaviour, saying that he was unaware that Max had any children or was ever married, but admitted that the resemblance was so uncanny that it took him by surprised. He thought for a moment that he was seeing a young Max. He ushered Gary into his office and offered beverages. While Gerard was out of the office getting the coffee Gary had requested, Gary could hear some idle chatter coming from the adjoining offices.

"You are the spitting image of your father," Gerard said as he returned with the coffee. "You even sound like him. Where is the old devil?"

"My father is missing," Gary replied.

Gerard let out a giggle, but stopped suddenly and asked, "What do you mean, missing?"

"He's been missing for nearly a year now," Gary said. "This is why I'm here in Africa looking for him."

"That cannot be," Gerard replied. "He was here six months ago when he picked up his dividend."

"What dividend?" Gary asked.

"This property. He owns over half of it."

"I was under the impression that he had sold his share," Gary said.

"Who told you that?"

"I heard it somewhere."

"That's not right," said Gerard. "About eight years ago, an acquaintance of his, a cashew farmer near Tanga in the state of Tanganyika, got himself into trouble through drinking. He borrowed money from the bank and could not make the repayment and knowing that the bank was about to foreclose on him and that he would be thrown off his land leaving his wife and two young children homeless, your father stepped in, bought the property and allowed him to stay and run it for him, but after a year he still would not stop drinking, his wife eventually left him, his dependency on alcohol increased and could no longer work, so your father had to go and personally manage the property.

"Not wanting to be managing both places, he offered me the opportunity to buy him out. Not being able to raise that kind of money, we came to an agreement that he would become a silent partner of the estate and collect a cash dividend twice a year. In fact, the dividend is again due and he personally picks it up here, so we expect to see him any day now. I can verify that with the accountant if you want me to."

"How much cash was the dividend, he last collected?" Gary asked.

"Look, I really cannot divulge that, but I can tell you it is in the thousands."

Gerard called for the accountant. A young Indian man appeared, and Gerard asked him to bring in the Blue Peter.

Not aware of the term 'Blue Peter', Gary was not sure of what they were talking about, but soon realised when the accountant appeared with a large cash book, that it meant a cash ledger.

Written in the ledger, halfway down the page, were two amounts and an initial next to them, his father's initials, Gary could see. Both numbers were in the several thousands.

"This is what you've been giving my father?" asked Gary.

"That's right."

Gary whistled softly and turned the ledger back to Gerard.

They talked about Gerard's memories of Gary's father for a while longer. Before Gary left, he gave Gerard Karen's contact number, saying that he could be contacted by leaving a message at that number should any new developments regarding his Dad arise, thanked him and left.

He stopped at the first telephone exchange and made a reverse charge call to Karen to tell her of the latest news. She sounded excited and told him that she would book a couple of rooms at the Tsavo Lodge, one room for two nights, and one for one night and get Asmani accommodation nearby. Meanwhile, she would make some enquiries about Gerard and drive up the following morning.

After getting Asmani settled at a hotel in Voi, and given him enough money for his meals, he pulled in at the Tsavo Lodge. The manager either being very observant and remembered him from his previous visit, or maybe from Karen making the bookings through her office, somehow associated Gary as being part of the law enforcement group and gave him special treatment.

"If the room does not suit you Sir, we will gladly move you to another," he said.

Here we go again, Gary thought, *it's not what you know, but who you know,* and pretended that he did not hear. Everyone should be given the same treatment, despite your creed, colour or religious belief, he had always believed, but he realised that he didn't live in a perfect world.

After a well needed shower and shave, he dressed in a casual shirt and slack, went down to the deck overlooking the water hole and sat at the same table at which he and Karen had previously sat and ordered a beer. The waiter soon appeared with a bottle of Tiger beer and a bowl of assorted salty nuts, poured the beer into a chilled glass and left. Gary spent another hour enjoying the scenery before heading to the dining room for dinner.

The restaurant was fairly busy with American tourists on a two day tour of the Park. They were having a wonderful time loudly exchanging exaggerated stories about the day's events.

On his way out of the dining room Gary spotted the Police Superintendent standing at the bar and talking to a couple of what seemed to be plain clothes detectives from the Crime Investigation Branch. He tried to avoid being seen, but the eagle-eyed Superintendent obviously trained in seeing faces, did not miss him. He quickly called out to Gary to come over and meet a couple of his detectives. He asked about Karen and made Gary promise that if they stayed in Voi for another night, he and his wife would be honoured to have them at their place for dinner. Gary promised to pass on the message.

The following morning, he was up and showered by seven, again having a coffee on the observation deck looking over the waterhole while waiting for Karen to arrive and have breakfast with him.

Looking as elegant as ever, she drove into the car park an hour later. She walked straight to the corner table where he was sitting, greeted him with a loving kiss, ordered breakfast and sat down to exchange their news.

Her investigation into Gerard's business had not resulted in anything unusual, his name appeared only as a manager/shareholder, in a company registered as the Coast Sisal Estate. All its taxes were up to date and the records also revealed that Gary's father was the major shareholder and decisions on all matters needed his approval and signature. Karen was puzzled by how the place was being run during his absence.

She insisted on driving to the estate, talking to Gerard and possibly interviewing some of the long-serving staff to make sure that all the stories checked out.

With breakfast completed and with Asmani in the back seat, they drove to the sisal estate in the Internal Security Land Rover. When they reached Gerard's office, he showed some sign of resentment when he discovered that Karen was from Internal Security. He could not understand why such a high profile department would get involved in a civil matter. The assurances from Gary that she was a personal friend helping him failed to put his mind at ease.

"How was that money paid to Gary's father?" she asked Gerard.

"Some was in cash, the rest was paid as several cheques made out to cash," he said.

"Which bank was used?"

"Our bank, the National Grindlays Bank," he replied.

Karen wrote that down in her diary, and also the numbers of the four cash cheques for the sum of four thousand shillings each that were issued to Gary's father.

"Something does not add up here," she said to Gary as they drove away from the Estate on their way to Voi Police Station, to talk to the Superintendent.

"What?" he asked.

"He was being evasive in his answers, I don't think he was telling the truth."

"And?"

"I'm going to dig deeper into the affairs of that company," she said with a smile. "Isn't this fun?"

"Hmmmm," said Gary and concentrated on the road.

She was greeted with uttermost respect at the police station and escorted straight to the Superintendent's office. She discussed her concerns with him and he promised to assign one of his detectives to investigate the matter immediately. She thanked him for the dinner invitation, but had to decline because she had other commitments. She would love to have dinner with him and his wife on her next visit, if the offer was still open, she said.

"It sure will be," the Superintendent replied.

After leaving the station, she talked Gary into coming back to Mombasa for a few days, where they would do further searches through the public records.

On the way down, Gary told Asmani that as he would be staying in Mombasa for a week, so he should take the opportunity to visit his family, with which Asmani seemed very pleased. Gary handed him twenty shillings which he was hesitant to take at first, but succumbed to Gary's persistence.

Back at Karen's place, Gary called Anthony to ask about his wife and daughter's progress and Anthony assured him that they were well on their way to full recovery.

"How are things going with you, has anything new surfaced?" Anthony asked.

He sounded concerned about Gary's difficulties in finding his father. Gary didn't want to go into any details as he was well aware that Karen kept Anthony constantly updated, but he said that he was making headway.

Karen spoke to the Superintendent at Voi early during the week and he too had not been able to uncover a great deal on Mr Gerard, but assured Karen that his detectives were on it. Other sources did not find too much either. It seemed that most of the dealings were done through Gary's father, so avoiding Gerard's name being scrutinised by the relevant authorities. Nothing further developed during the week.

Karen had arranged for them to spend a couple of days at her weekender by the sea. So Gary spent the morning buying fishing lines, hooks, sinkers, bait and a pair of swimming trunks while Karen organised provisions. Early that Friday afternoon, they drove to the ramp and took their car across on the Likoni Ferry and within the hour they were at their destination.

Gary helped Karen with the chores required to get the house functioning, turning on the fridge, opening the window slats and airing out the place, spraying for bugs, unpacking the food, making the bed and sweeping out the wooden floors and verandas.

With the tasks out of the way, they walked barefoot along the white sandy beach, close enough to the water's edge to get their feet wet by the gentle waves as it rolled ashore, and enjoyed the coolness of the afternoon sea breeze as it gently brushed past them. For Gary, it brought back memories of his beloved Seychelles that made him realise how much he had missed being one with the sea. Silently he sat for a moment lost in his thoughts returning him back to his childhood and pondering other exotic destinations that lay beyond.

The silence was broken by a group of seagulls squawking over a scrap of food they were attempting to extract from the water. It being too heavy to lift, they kept dropping it back into the surf while making a loud racket trying to retrieve it. The sight kept him amused for a while.

The events of the last few months had profoundly affected them both and they found the tranquillity of these surroundings to be extremely therapeutic.

They spent the next two days swimming, fishing and enjoying each other's company. That night Karen brought up the inevitable subject, about their relationship and age differences, a subject Gary had often thought about but chosen to ignore.

Karen, being a practical girl, explained to him that their love although strong now, may not last forever.

Not prepared to face the fact that age could influence their relationship, he refused to go into any further discussion on the matter, stating that love would conquer all.

"That should not stop us from seeing each other now," she said. "We should make a promise that if and when the time comes, we will always remain friends."

Gary on the other hand could not bring himself to think of what life would be without Karen, and asked, "Are you trying to break off with me?"

She laughed and said, "No, my darling I love you too much to do that, but we have to be realistic."

Gary felt all empty inside, although she kept reassuring him that she would be with him for as long as he wanted her and would stay his friend beyond that, it still made him feel uneasy.

They drove back to Karen's house late Sunday night, both exhausted from their weekend adventure. As Karen had an early start the following day, they decided to have an early night.

By the time he woke the next day she had already left for work.

Chapter 33

Karen called mid-morning and arranged to meet at her office. He arrived within the hour.

She told him that the Voi detectives had found his Dad's car parked in a shed at the Sisal plantation. Gerard said that he had left it there when he purchased the Land Rover and that had been confirmed by the staff. Karen found it hard to understand why Gerard had kept that information from them.

She rang the Superintendent to thank him for his speedy action. He assured her that he had assigned two of his best detectives to the case and would keep her updated daily.

"What do we do now?" Gary asked.

"We have the wheels in motion," said Karen, "and we wait for a few days to see the outcome. Meanwhile, I've made an appointment for us to meet with the manager of the National Grindlays Bank at 3.00 pm, but right now we need to keep our strength up by having a bite to eat."

Gary nodded his approval as they walked down to the local restaurant that Karen often frequented.

The Bank Manager was a very astute English

gentleman in his late forties or early fifties. The bank account was held under the company's name of Coast Sisal Estate. The manager brought out the records and although not showing them to Gary because of privacy laws, gave any information that they asked. The account had three registered signatories, which were Gary's Dad, Gerard and the accountant. However, only two signatures were required at any one time on any of the cheques.

Karen showed him the cheque numbers for the four thousand shillings amount each, asking him to verify if any of them had been cashed. He left and returned a little while later with a statement stating that one had been cashed at a National Grindlays Bank in the state of Uganda nine weeks ago. He also told them that for a Bank to cash a cheque of this size, they would need the person's name, address, driving license, or passport and of course his signature and he could have that information sent down within a week.

Karen asked that it be done.

They left the bank bewildered, but confident that they were making progress. Karen laughed and said, "When we finally crack this, you and I should join forces and start a private investigating business."

"We're a good team, I agree," said Gary.

With another week of waiting, Gary decided to drive to Malindi and tell Asmani of the outcome, so saving him the unnecessary travel back.

The following morning he left on the drive and later met and had lunch with Asmani's family. Gary was made to promise that he would call on Asmani as soon as he was ready to resume the search. He drove back to Mombasa later that day.

Very little development occurred during the next few days. The letter with the information had arrived at the bank and the ID and signatures proved to be those of his father.

"Uganda is a long way away," said Karen. "The one thing to our advantage is that being one of the East African States, it comes under Anthony's jurisdiction."

Worried about letting him go alone on such a long trip into the unknown, she decided to call Anthony and arrange for her to take some time off work and accompany him.

Being in a meeting, Anthony was not able to take her call, but within half an hour had got back to her. She brought him up to date with the latest development, asked for some leave. Anthony agreed with her, at the same time saying that she would be more help if she accompanied him in an official capacity.

"I don't want to abuse the system," she said. "Wouldn't that be a bit outside regulations?"

"Leave me to worry about regulations," said Anthony. "Now, I'll make the necessary arrangements with my Kampala office. Good luck and give Gary my regards. "Don't forget to keep me updated." Without further words, he hung up.

Chapter 34

The flight to Uganda was a long one, but being a seasoned traveller of all of two flights, Gary showed none of the fear he had displayed on his maiden voyage. They had to switch flights in Nairobi and take a smaller plane to Uganda. During the trip, he was given a tour of the cockpit at Karen's request.

Karen spent most of the journey working on some case files while Gary enjoyed the views especially crossing the escarpment and of Lake Victoria, that resembled an ocean. Four hours after leaving Mombasa, they made their descent over the lake and landed at Entebbe Airport in Uganda, about twenty miles from the capital, Kampala.

The city is built on the shores of Lake Victoria, the world's second largest fresh water lake, and the source of the River Nile. The city is surrounded by seven hills and it is also known as Africa's greenest and best designed city.

As they drove in by taxi, they looked in fascination at the sights. The colonial buildings looked freshly painted in white and seemed Victorian in style. The strongly British appearance also showed in the tree lined streets and the flower gardens dotted along the entire city streets and parks, giving it the look of a modern painting. The air was fresh and nippy as evening approached.

Their room at the Grand Imperial Hotel on Nile Road gave them an uninterrupted view over the lake.

Although late, that evening after they had settled, they decided to spend at least an hour in investigative work, starting with the hotel register. After talking to the hotel manager, they were shown to an office and the large, leather-bound book was brought to them. They looked as far back as four weeks but could not see Gary's Dad's name in the Grand Imperial registry.

They went to the lounge area where an open warm wood fire was burning and ordered drinks, settled in armchairs and thought deeply about Gary's father's possible next move. Unaware of their surroundings, they were brought back to the room when they heard a voice from behind them.

"Inspector Willis?"

Karen turned around and saw a tall, well-dressed man with dark hair staring at her.

"Yes?" she replied.

"I am Sergeant Jack Andrews," the newcomer said.

"Hi!" said Karen, getting to her feet as they shook hands

"The boss's descriptions of you both were perfect. And I take it you are Gary?" he said, as he turned and faced Gary who had also risen from the armchair

"Hello, Jack," Gary replied, shaking his hand.

"I've heard and read about you," said the sergeant.

"I hope all good things," Gary replied.

"Yes, I assure you."

Both men laughed.

"I've been assigned to assist you for the next two days," said Andrews.

"Will you join us for a drink?" asked Gary.

"My pleasure," said Andrews and took a third armchair as the other two resumed theirs. "Scotch, please."

Gary waved at the waiter and they waited until it had been brought.

"Let me bring you up to date," said Karen and spent ten minutes giving Andrews as complete a picture of the search for the missing man as she could.

Andrews listened intently and finally nodded.

"How about I pick you up at 8:30 tomorrow morning?" he said.

"Sounds good," said Gary and Karen nodded.

Andrews finished his drink, stood up and said, "See you tomorrow." With that, he left.

"Dinner, I think," said Gary and they made their way to the restaurant to sample the local cuisine.

After dinner they put on a warm jacket each, and took an evening stroll along the lake foreshore.

After being picked up by Sergeant Andrews in the morning, they first visited the bank where the four thousand shilling cheque had been cashed. They were ushered into the manager's office and Andrews asked to speak directly to the teller who had cashed the cheque. After waiting for almost ten minutes, the manager returned with the lady concerned. She looked a little concerned at first but when Karen reassured her that she had done nothing wrong, she seemed to relax.

"Can you remember cashing the cheque?" asked Karen.

"I can, yes," the teller replied.

"And you checked all the necessary details?"

"Of course. He showed me his passport and gave me a sample signature as well as his driving licence to confirm his name and address. I asked the accountant to double-check and he approved the details."

"Can you remember what he looked like?" asked Gary.

The woman though for a few moments.

"Elderly," said at last. "Maybe fifties and very well dressed in a smart safari suit like most Western men wear."

"Was he alone?" asked Andrews.

"I can't remember," the woman said. "It was a busy morning and there were quite a lot of people in the line. I can't be sure if anyone was with him."

"I want you to think very hard," said Andrews, leaning quite close to her in a rather intimidating way. "Was there anyone next to him when the cheque was cashed?"

The technique clearly didn't work, as the teller flinched and became nervous, shaking her head.

Andrews abandoned the approach, handed her his business card and asked her to call him should she remember anything else about the man.

Thanking the bank manager for his help, they left.

They visited three more hotels before lunch and again examined the visitor registries but without success. Having the extra help expedited their search. Jack Andrews took them to a restaurant right on the lake front for lunch, where they both ordered grilled Lake Victoria's cod fillets and salad.

For the afternoon they planned to inspect the registers of another seven hotels and resorts. The fourth place was a resort on one of the hills, with a distant view of the lake. The owner, a young, attractive woman in her thirties confirmed that the gentleman in the photograph was the same person who stayed at the hotel and admitted that he looked much older than the photograph. He was accompanied by a slim brunette lady possibly ten years or so younger than he was. They stayed for five days and registered under the name of Mr and Mrs Bernard. She showed them the register. She also confirmed that they were driving a white Land Rover with a Kenyan registration plate and settled their account in cash.

The information brought a smile to their faces.

"That explains the secrecy of it all," said Gary. "Now we may have to go back and find out whose wife may be missing from amongst his friends or acquaintances."

To be totally certain, Andrews took away the page from the hotel register where the guests had signed in as Mr and Mrs Bernard.

"I'll have the hand writing analysed by an expert," he said. "Hopefully, that could be done by tomorrow. Look, I'll have to spend the afternoon doing office work. Why don't you take the departmental car to take in the sites of Kampala?"

"That's very generous," said Karen. "Call us at the hotel this evening and we can compare notes."

After dropping Andrews back at his office, they toured all of the seven hills, visited the government house and its gardens and drove along Lake Victoria, visiting several villages occupied by the Luo Tribes. At a tea house in the visitors' centre in one of the villages, they met a young Luo girl employed as a tour guide who related the history and customs of her tribe.

One of their customs that Both Gary and Karen found fascinating was that when a man dies, his brother inherits the wife and must treat her as his own. And if he does not have a brother, then she goes to the nearest relative.

"Once that person is dead, the spirit stays with the wife and can create a bad omen," said the guide. "To avoid that, the wife must sleep with another man within a set time."

Finding it hard to understand that custom, Gary asked Karen,

"What would happen if you did not like the women"?

They both laughed;

Leaving the centre, they then drove up a hill and watched the sun setting over the lake, before returning Andrews' car to his office.

Meanwhile, Andrew had sent out a circular to all the hotels and resorts in Uganda to see if the Bernard name and registration had been documented elsewhere.

Back at their hotel room, they freshened up and went to the lounge for a well-deserved drink.

They were introduced by the hotel manager to a group of photographers and film makers doing a documentary on gorillas, and chimpanzees. They had just returned after spending ten days in the forest amongst the primates. Their stories were so enthralling that they kept Gary and Karen entertained for a good hour or so, but eventually they had to excuse themselves and make a quick dash for the dining room that was about to close.

Although exhausted, they were confident that their day had been a successful one and they were looking forward to the result from the hand writing expert the following day.

The morning found them totally rested and ready for the new day's challenge. At just after 10:00, Andrews called and confirmed that the hand writing results were positive, which brought some joy to Gary confirming that his Dad was fine.

But new questions had surfaced; who was he with, where was he heading to, and still why the secrecy?

Andrews rang the check post on the Congo / Uganda border to ask them to keep a lookout for that particular vehicle but to his surprise was told that the post had been unmanned for over eight months, when all restrictions on entry into the Congo had been lifted.

With no further need to remain in Uganda, they made their way to the airport to return to Mombasa. Entebbe airport was very quiet when they arrived; there were only twelve passengers on the flight, on a plane that could carry over thirty. The airline could not guarantee them a joining flight to Mombasa that same afternoon; however luck turned their way on arrival at Nairobi Airport, they managed to get a connecting flight and were home late that night.

Chapter 35

For several days after their return, Gary noticed that Karen was starting work extra early and finishing late every day and was also taking extra work home with her. He felt that she was spending too much time helping him and had to put in the extra hours to catch up with her own work, although she would not admit it.

To allow her time to catch up, he decided to make arrangements with Asmani to go back to Malindi and do some fishing at the place where they had previously caught the crabs and lobsters. He told Karen when she arrived home that evening.

Not wanting him to wander too far away, she suggested that he used her beach house with the condition that she would join him on Friday and they would spend the weekend together. She assured him that the area also contained a great abundance of fish, crabs and lobsters. Not wanting to put her under further stress, he agreed and planned to leave the following morning.

Karen rang the Superintendent at Voi to update him on the latest developments. After having digested it all, he concluded that Gerard from the Sisal Plantation knew more than he was revealing. He suggested that they apply additional pressure by getting his detectives to declare him as a suspect in Max's disappearance and hauling him in for questioning, in the hope that he would break down and tell them all he knew.

Around the same time, news arrived from Andrews in Kampala, saying that he had received information from the owner of the Lake Albert hotel that six days ago, a Mr and Mrs Bernard had spent two days at the hotel. The registration number of the vehicle was entered in the registry, although the owner could not confirm that his wife who booked them in had sighted the vehicle, and as she was away at the moment he could not confirm.

Karen rang Gary at her house hoping that she would catch him before he left. She was in luck he was just about to get in his car when Denise called out to him. Gary drove straight to Karen's office.

They discussed the possibility that his father might be heading for the Belgian Congo, and as he was fluent in French and the Congo being a French speaking state, he may have friends there to he was visiting.

On the wall in her office was a map of the whole of East Africa including details of all the roads, hotels, fuel stations, hospitals, police posts, post offices, all townships and more. Gary carefully studied it and came to the conclusion that at the pace and direction his father was travelling it didn't seem he was in any particular hurry to get anywhere specific.

Gary decided to fly to Kampala then hire a car and head towards Lake Albert and have a good chance of catching up with him somewhere along the way, or even before he reached the Congo and Ruandan Border, if that was where he was heading.

Karen booked him on the afternoon flight to Entebbe and arranged a car hire. She also contacted Sergeant Andrews and gave him Gary's arrival details.

Gary landed at Entebbe airport late that day and was surprised to find Andrews there to meet him. The sergeant had prepared a package that contained road conditions and maps. The shortest route to Lake Albert was clearly marked with accommodations along the way. Also in it was a letter of introduction to any police post along the way, instructing them to give any required assistance. He also insisted that Gary carry a hand gun and enough ammunition, which he already had in his travel bag, and to avoid travelling at night when wild animals roamed on or close to the highway, often causing fatal crashes.

Gary made arrangements with the concierge to give him a wakeup call at 3.00 a.m. so he could be on his way by 4.00 am.

Although well aware of the danger and driving cautiously to avoid colliding with nocturnal wild animals that were in abundance along the way, he still encountered some near misses. By sunrise he had left the Lake and was driving across the Mountain Pass of Western Uganda in his hired four cylinder Ford car.

Back down on the flat plains, the road was straight and desolated. He drove for well over two hours without coming across another vehicle or encountering another human being. But as he started the climb into the hills, the road became very windy and slowed his progress immensely.

At the bottom of the pass at a river crossing, he came

across a pride of lions and their cubs, sitting on the old wooden bridge enjoying the warmth of the morning sun. Even after several burst on the car horn, they took their time sauntering off the bridge, obviously not pleased at being disturbed.

Approaching a small village further west, there was a sign saying that it was the last fuel depot for the next two hundred miles. He decided to fuel up the car and the spare jerry can he was carrying and get enough provisions to last him for at least a week. Should the unforeseen happen or a break-down should occur, he intended to remain close to his vehicle until rescued.

He questioned the shopkeepers at several fuelling posts along the way regarding a white Land Rover and an elderly gentleman, but couldn't get any clear answers, as the language became a barrier as few of the natives in that part spoke Swahili.

He was making good progress and estimated that at the rate he was travelling he would reach his destination before night fall.

Driving along, enjoying the scenery, he came across an open field and saw a pack of chimpanzees with babies on their backs foraging for food. He pulled up and watched them for a while. It did not seem to bother them that he had stopped and some of the babies wondered over close to the car to investigate but then carried on playing as their parents went about their business.

At a small village near a lake, he came across a group of small people, walking along the road with bows and arrows strapped to their backs, carrying a dead animal resembling a monkey. Gary thought they were a bit young to be hunting on their own, but soon realised as he reached the village, that he was in Pygmy country and they were fully grown adults. They showed great excitement, waving as his car went past.

From the turn-off past the village, road conditions gradually deteriorated to the extent that made it impossible to avoid the gigantic pot holes that were appearing all over the highway and eventually he ended up with a blown tyre.

Worried about being attacked by either lions or leopards, he kept his hand gun within reach as he stepped out to change the damaged wheel with the spare. On completion, his hands were covered in mud and needed washing. He scanned the area for any danger before deciding to wash his hands in a stream that ran along the road. The water seemed so fresh and clean that he used some to wet his face as well.

Although realising that it would slow him down, he had no alternative but to reduce speed and take extra care to avoid damaging another tyre which would have left him stranded.

He reached his destination at the police post late in the night. With no sign of life around, he decided to park his car in front of the police post and sleep in it. A woollen blanket knitted by the women of the Luo Tribes that he had purchased for Karen at a village shop on one of his stops came in handy. He unpacked it and wrapped it around him and it kept him warm right through the night.

He was woken up early the following morning by the loud rattling noises coming from a truck transporting drums of fuel and lubricants, heading towards the Congo border.

He got out of his hired car and wondered over to the Police Post to use the toilet. On his return he met a young Askari who was about to open the station. Gary showed his badge and asked for his senior officer. The Askari suddenly showed extra alertness, invited him into the building, offered him tea and called the senior officer. He replaced the phone and told Gary that the corporal would arrive within ten minutes.

The corporal arrived on foot exactly on time. Gary introduced himself and handed over the letter from Andrews. The corporal read it and as protocol demanded, made a call to Andrews in Kampala to confirm Gary's arrival.

To Gary's dismay, he received the exact treatment he had received from the Askaries at the Taveta Taita Police Post. Being a white officer, even though only a reserve, automatically gave him seniority.

The corporal was a huge jovial Luo man, obviously out of condition mostly because not much ever happened in this part of the country to keep up his fitness. He seemed to have complete control over his domain, as the station looked extremely well maintained and clean. He was a very pleasant man, with great personality and showed real authority towards his juniors. He offered to have his wife cook Gary eggs for breakfast. Having eaten boiled eggs that were readily available along all the village stops, Gary declined stating he would prefer a piece of bread and jam and another cup of coffee if at all possible.

The coffee was so bitter that he needed four spoons of sugar to be able to digest it and the bread although recently baked, was only palatable after being dunked in the coffee.

They discussed a plan of action and the corporal suggested placing an instant road block on the main road in front of the police post, and have it manned twenty four hours a day for the next few days. He would contact other nearby posts to have them keep an eye for the white Land Rover. Apart from the occasional trucks, there would have been fewer than five cars using the highway each day.

Gary was given accommodation in the officer's quarters at the post that was serviced daily by the sergeant's wife. Electricity was generated from the town power supplies between 6.00 pm and 9.00pm daily, the only fridge around was a kerosene operated fridge at the police post where some medicines and other small perishable essentials were kept.

Gary felt that he was wasting precious time hanging around but without a spare tyre, his travel was restricted.

Three days passed without even sighting a white Land Rover and other police posts that the corporal had contacted, returned the same verdict. The only other positive news was that the Congo border had been closed for well over two weeks, due to the main bridge having been washed away during the recent flood, and would not be re-opened for months. And that would only leave entry into Ruanda, which his father would not be heading for, as the country was facing civil unrest.

Gary figured that his father, if he was really the person travelling under that name, might well be on his way home via a different route. He therefore decided to head back as soon as his tyre arrives.

He was a little under the weather with a stomach ache, when the local garage delivered his wheel late that afternoon.

Not feeling all that well, he decided to skip dinner. During the night he became nauseous, and the cramp and pain in his stomach kept him up the entire night, his condition worsened the following day. With no medical facilities within two hundred miles, the town residents depended mainly on the natural medicine when sick, and when things got worse, their local witch doctor for their cure.

Gary was left with no other alternative but to wait and hope for the best. The corporal although possessing a first aid certificate, did not have any medicine on hand to administer. By the afternoon, Gary could not even hold down a cup of black tea and had dehydrated to such an extent that his stomach felt like it was on fire. Hoping that he had contracted a stomach bug that would eventually get better, he stayed in bed. By night time he was having unbearable cramps in his stomach. The corporal's wife brought him some infused bitter native herbs to drink in the hope of easing the pain. He was feeling so ill that he did not hesitate taking it, he figured that the herbal drink would either kill or cure him. He classed both options as a remedy.

On the sixth day although still weak, the pain had eased. He tried to place a call to Karen's office in Mombasa to inform her of his decision to return, but was told that the phone line had been down for a couple of days. He asked the corporal to advise Sergeant Andrews in Kampala that he was on his way back, as soon as the phone line was repaired.

As weak as he felt, he threw his few belongings loosely on the back seat, and thanked the corporal for his help, before setting out on his long trip back. Driving at a much slower pace to avoid another tyre failure, he headed back making frequent rest stops. After having been on the road for nine hours, avoiding collisions with animals feeding along the highway, he finally pulled in at a village shop that were about to shut.

The burning pain in his stomach had eased but he remained so weak that he could hardly stand up. Not wanting to drink water that may have been the cause for his sickness, he staggered into the shop and purchased a bottle of lemonade and a packet of aspirin

Back in his car he drank the lemonade and swallowed two of the tablets and sat for another ten minutes before resuming his journey.

A few miles further he came across an old run-down motel, which in normal circumstances he would have gone past, but realising that he could not go any further, he turned in and booked a room for the night. He managed to get into the room before collapsing on the bed.

Chapter 36

The receptionist at the desk of the Splendid Hotel in Mombasa was new and she didn't recognise the fit, healthy-looking middle-aged man accompanied by an elegant, well-dressed woman as they checked in. She gave them the room key and touched the bell to call a porter to carry their bags.

"Will you be staying long, sir?" she asked politely, noting that they had booked in for just three days.

"That depends on the airlines," the man said. "We're going to head up to France as soon as we can and visit Elise's parents. We were supposed to be in the Congo now, but the road's been closed for weeks after the floods."

"Yes, I'd heard about the floods," the receptionist replied. "I'm sure our travel agent can help you with your bookings."

"The bank first," said the man. "Then we'll talk to the agent."

The young porter arrived and the receptionist said, "Take Mr and Mrs Bernard to Room 303."

A few minutes later, having tipped the porter, the two laughed.

"They assumed we're husband and wife!" Elise said and opened the fridge door to check on the liquor supplies.

"This is a very conservative place," Max replied, pointing at the bottle of beer. "They'd probably chuck us out if they knew!"

Finishing the cold beer in two gulps, Max kissed her on the cheek. "Back in just a tick," he said. "I'll go and organise the travellers' cheques, then we can talk to the agent about the flight to Paris."

"I'll get the bags unpacked," she replied as he left the room.

Max was unprepared for the reception he got at the bank.

"Mr Max Bernard!" exclaimed the teller at the counter. "We've been worried about you!"

"Eh? Worried? What the hell for?"

"Let me get the manager," the teller said and moved rapidly to the office at the back, emerging a few moments later to lead Max in through the gate between the counters and the public area and to the office. He opened the door and ushered Max inside.

The bank manager rose to his feet as he entered. He was the same man Max had dealt with on his last visit, a short man, greyish hair, wearing the standard, light-weight cotton suit, open at the neck and no tie that most well to do men wore in Africa. Two yellow nicotine stained fingers on his right hand revealed a chain smoker.

"Mr Bernard!" he said. "I'm most relieved to see you!" He took Max's hand and shook it enthusiastically.

"You're the second person to say that!" said Max, taking a seat across from the manager's desk. "What the hell's going on?"

The manager took his own seat. "You've been missing for months," he said.

"Missing? I haven't been missing! Good grief, can't a man go travelling without reporting in every day?"

"Of course, you can, but your son has been here for some months now, looking for you. And the Security Forces have joined in the search also."

"What?" Max stared at him. "Gary? Here? What the hell for? I'd written to him before I set off to tell him what I was doing. I gave a bunch of the letters to my partner Gerard at the Estate to mail off to him. How long has he been here?"

"Close to a year. As soon as he arrived in Kenya he was enlisted in the Kenya Regiment to do his National Service."

Max was thunderstruck. "Well, I imagine that did the kid the world of good and made him grow up pretty damned quick! Where is he now?"

"I don't know. But I think you had better contact the police right away."

Max seemed to be taking some time to recover his composure.

"Yes, I will," he said, taking an envelope from his jacket pocket. "But can you get this organised for me? I'm heading to France as soon as I can and I need travellers' cheques. Here's a list of the denominations I want. Will you arrange it?"

"Of course, Mr Bernard. Drop in tomorrow morning, I'll have them ready. Now if I may suggest... the police?"

"On my way," said Max as got to his feet and walked out.

* * *

"Max Bernard," he announced to the duty officer behind the counter at the police station. "I believe you're looking for me."

The constable stared at him. "Indeed we are, Mr Bernard! Where have you been?"

"Travelling," said Max. "I didn't realise I was supposed to keep everybody advised of my itinerary." His irritation was growing.

"Actually, Mr Bernard, we do strongly recommend just that," the constable replied. "The way things have been going here with the Mau Mau insurgency, travelling alone is not recommended. Are you staying here now?"

"I'm at the Splendid for a couple of days."

"I know that Intelligence wants to talk to you. I'll have somebody contact you at the hotel."

"Okay, do that," said Max and walked out.

The constable picked up the phone.

* * *

Karen was deep into routine reports when the phone rang.

"Inspector Willis," she said.

"Mombasa Police Station, Ma'am," said the constable. "Mr Bernard has just reported in. He had no idea we were looking for him. He's at the Splendid."

"Thank you officer," she replied controlling the shock and replaced the phone. "Good grief!" she said to the empty chairs in her office, stood up and raced down to the car park.

* * *

She knocked on the door of Room 303 and waited, struggling to control her nerves. When the door opened, she was disappointed to see a woman.

"Inspector Willis?" the woman said. Her French accent was strong. "The police said you were coming. I'm Elise Pelletier. Please come in. Max is just in the bathroom."

"Thank you." Karen walked in and stood in the middle of the spacious room. A large double bed stood against one wall, there were four chairs around a coffee table and a huge floor to ceiling window gave a wonderful view out over the city.

Elise sat in one of the chairs but Karen remained standing, nerves jangling through her body. The sound of the toilet flushing broke the silence, a man's cough came from the bathroom and the door opened. Max walked into the room, looking apprehensive.

"Inspector Willis? I hear you're looking for me?"

She stared at him. "You do look a lot like Gary," she said.

"You know my son?" He looked startled.

"We've been friends since he came to Kenya. I've been helping him with the search."

"God, I haven't seen the kid in a decade. He was just a fragile little boy then."

"And now he's a tall, handsome man who looks a lot like you. And he's got quite a reputation with Intelligence for his work against the Mau Mau."

"Good grief! It's hard to believe. And where is Gary now, Inspector Willis?"

"Karen, please. He's on his way back from Uganda and the Congo border."

"Uganda? What the hell was he doing there?"

"Looking for you. You must have been there at one point."

"We were. We've been travelling a bit, first chance I've had since I came to Kenya. But I don't understand, why the fuss? He knew where I was."

"How could he, Mr Bernard?   He and his mother hadn't heard from you for well over a year."

"What? No, that's wrong, I'd written letters to them, Gerard at the Estate was supposed to have posted them."

"Then I think Gerard has some questions to answer. No letters have been delivered."

Max went silent for a few moments, apparently digesting this news.

"When is Gary due back here?" he finally asked.

"I don't know," she said. "We know he left by car, but we've not been able to contact him for a day or two. I'll go back to my office and see what I can find out from the local stations.   You won't leave Mombasa for a few days, I hope?"

"How could I, with my son missing somewhere between Kampala and here?"

"I'll call you when I get news," said Karen and walked out of the hotel room. She drove back to her office and picked up the phone.

* * *

"Kampala Police."

"This is Inspector Karen Willis in Mombasa. Put me through to Sergeant Andrews."

"Stand by, Ma'am."

"Sergeant Andrews. Good morning, ma'am."

"Sergeant, any news on Gary?"

"Nothing, ma'am. I'll call Lake Albert, see if they've heard anything."

"Do that, Sergeant. If you make contact, tell him his father has just shown up in Mombasa."

"Good god! He has? Is he okay?"

"He's been travelling."

Andrews was silent for a moment.

"I'll call you as soon as I hear anything," he said.

Half an hour later, he called her back.

"Inspector Willis, I talked to the Lake Albert Post. They said Gary had left yesterday, but he was suffering from a stomach bug, he really was unwell, so he was moving slowly. But there have been no reports of accidents, so I'd say he's just going slow, though I suppose there could be a breakdown or an accident. I've called the stations along the road to keep an eye open for him."

"Thank you, Sergeant," said Karen and hung up. She was getting seriously worried.

Gary woke early the following morning still feeling weak. His whole body had bite marks from either mosquitoes or bed bugs he was not sure. He knew that he could not survive another night in that room. He made himself a cup of coffee and forced it down, glad that it stayed down. He even felt too weak to have a shower. He dressed, staggered to his car and drove out.

He arrived at the village of Mityana near Lake Wamala mid-morning, pulled in at the village shop, had his car refuelled and purchased a packet of dry biscuits and another bottle of lemonade. With only fifty miles to Kampala, and still eight hours of day light remaining, he drove on.

Ten miles down the road on a mountain pass, a speeding truck came at him from the wrong side of the road. As he swerved to avoid a head on collision, his vehicle skidded and went down an embankment and came to rest against a couple of trees eighty yards down.

Gary was thrown out of the car as it barrelled down the hill, and made heavy contact with a clump of trees and finally landed on a rock ledge rendering him unconscious.

Later that day, a young couple travelling west stopped at a lookout to take photos of the sunset. They noticed a set of tyre tracks, and some debris on the mountain pass indicating that a vehicle might have gone over the edge a few miles east of Mityana. With dusk approaching, it was difficult to see far enough down the valley. They decided to inform the authorities at the nearest police post on their way west, which happened to be at the Village of Mubende, forty miles away

Having been told by Andrews about Gary's condition, Karen was concerned to the point of booking herself a seat on the first available flight to Kampala, which was late the following afternoon. She spent the night pacing up and down staring at the phone at her every turn as if expecting it to ring at any instant. Her mother although trying extremely hard to get her to settle, finally decided on giving her two sleeping tablets that eventually sent her into a deep sleep.

Appearing in her dream was Gary leaning on the railing of her veranda against this backdrop of the most beautiful sunrise she had ever witnessed. But as quickly as it had appeared, it turned into a dull sunset. As she ran out to greet him, he simply vanished.

She leaped out of bed, and let out a screech. Afraid that Karen was being attacked, Denise ran to her room. Karen's face had a look of terror that Denise had never seen before. Not knowing whether the sleeping tablet was the cause or the effect of a nightmare and of what medicine to give her, she grabbed the first thing she came across on the side board, which happened to be a bottle of brandy that had been sitting there for a couple of years. Without fully realising what she was doing, she grabbed a glass and poured some in it, and gave it to Karen. She took one gulp and after a few loud coughs, regained her composure but the apprehensive look remained. She kept yelling out that something had happened to Gary.

"You were having a bad dream, everything is fine, he will be here tomorrow," Denise assured her.

But Karen could not stop sobbing. Denise sensed that something was definitely wrong and she was powerless to do anything.

Karen spent the rest of the night sitting on the veranda, staring out at the harbour lights, something they had often done together, trying hard to figure out what the dream was telling her. Although she tried hard to avoid the negative thought, she sensed that Gary was in need of help and all she wanted was to be by his side, even though she realised that it was impossible.

Chapter 37

The police were at the scene right on day break. They found the vehicle wedged between two trees, about hundred yards down the embankment. With the damp condition prevailing from the cold night, access was difficult and dangerous but eventually they managed to make their way down to the car. Although a lot of blood was found in and around the vehicle, no occupants were found in or near it. Further search resulted in nothing else being seen.

They called their Kampala police department to get the registration number matched to the owner and returned to their station to await further instruction.

After confirming that the vehicle was a rental and that Internal Security had been seeking information regarding it, a call was waiting for Andrews as he arrived at his office. He stood motionless trying to figure his next move, wondering whether to call Karen or drive out to the scene first.

Distressed, he chose the latter and arrived at the scene ninety minutes later. The cause of the accident was established to be possibly tiredness, or the icy road condition and upon further search, they found the body in a ravine another hundred yards further down.

It was established that the driver was thrown out of the car during the accident and later attempted to crawl back up to reach the highway for help, somehow slipped and fell a further eighty yards down the gorge.

Although very traumatized, Andrews realised that he must personally tell Karen. On a couple of occasions he replaced the receiver while starting to dial her number, not knowing how best to tell her. Eventually after practising his lines, he gathered enough courage to let it ring through.

Frightened and tensely waiting for the call, she answered on the first ring.

"Hello, Karen here," she said.

"It's Jack Andrews," he managed to say.

There was a long silence. He could not bring himself to tell her and she on the other hand did not want to hear. But between the silence and trembles in his voice, he managed to give her the news.

Karen went into shock and dropped the phone. Denise managed to get her to her bed and called the doctor who administered some sedatives that managed to put her to sleep.

Andrews then rang Anthony's office to inform him, and he too was deeply shocked. Anthony went home, gathered a few clothes and told his wife that he had to make an urgent trip to Mombasa, but would not give the reason.

Meanwhile with all the commotion going on, Gary's father had not been informed about the accident, and Karen being the only one who knew of his whereabouts was oblivious to it all, causing Denise to be concerned.

By late afternoon Anthony had arrived and taken control of the situation and made all the legal arrangements for flying the body to Mombasa and the funeral and the whole list of steps that had to be followed.

Feeling the awfulness of the situation, he knew that the next step was to see Gary's father. With dread in his heart, he went to his car and drove to the Hotel Splendid.

Max sat on the edge of the bed, almost collapsing, his body like a marionette with the strings cut. His face was white and occasional deep sobs erupted from him. Elise sat next to him, her arms round his shoulders, tears running down her cheeks.

Max took a deep breath, struggling for self-control.

"You were Gary's boss?"

"No sir, I'm Karen's boss. But Gary had performed so well with the KRP that we all felt we owed him something, so I made Karen available to help in the search."

Another deep sob came from Max. "I haven't seen him for ten years and then I miss him by a few days. He was a good soldier, you say?"

"The best, sir. His men would follow him anywhere and he personally rescued my wife and daughter from a bunch of terrorists."

"Do you have any photographs of him while he was here?"

"I do, sir." Anthony took the package of photos that he had got from Karen earlier and handed them to the older man who opened the package and stared at each of the pictures in turn. Some were of Gary in uniform, two of them were pictures of him and Karen together. Elise also looked at them.

"What a handsome son you had, Max," she whispered, wiping her eyes.

Max's shoulders shook a little. "This woman, that's Karen? The officer who was here before?"

"Yes, sir."

"Were they.... a pair?"

"They were very close. I think they might have got married in time."

"She looks a bit older than Gary."

"About four years, but she knew what a fine man he was, so it made no difference."

Carefully, Max put the pictures away as if knowing what was coming then he collapsed in a storm of weeping. Anthony and Elise exchanged glances and each knew what was being said.

"I'll advise the Seychelles Consulate in Mombasa," said Anthony. "And I'll send a telegram to Gary's mother. I have the address."

She nodded with a brief smile.

Anthony made for the door, knowing Elise would take care of Max.

Chapter 38

In all the grief and pain over Gary's death, one piece of information had stuck in Karen's mind.

Max Bernard had said he'd written letters to his ex-wife and his children to tell them he'd be travelling for some months. He'd left those letters with Gerard at the Estate with instructions to post them, but it appeared the instructions had been ignored.

Both the Superintendent and Karen intended to find the reason behind it.

"I'm coming with you," said Karen.

"Not a chance," replied the Superintendent. "This is a criminal matter, not State Security. Anyway, you're in no state to do this. You're too emotionally involved."

Accepting the inevitable, Karen nodded.

"You'll keep me informed?"

"Of course. Karen, go home and rest. You're a wreck."

After having made all the necessary arrangements, Anthony took a flight back to Nairobi to inform his wife and daughter. He did not want to tell them on the phone as he knew that they would take it badly. However, he asked

Jessica to have his grey suit ready and also to pack a few clothes for herself and Corrine as they would be away for a few days and he would update her with the rest on his return.

Jessica sensed that something was wrong by Anthony's strange behaviour. She confronted him as he entered the front door.

"What's happened?" she asked.

He hesitated.

"Tell me, *please,*" she insisted.

Anthony sat her down, and told her the whole story. Jessica sobbed through it then composed herself enough to go to her room pick up her travel case and call out to Corrine that it was time to leave.

The police car rolled up to the office of the Sisal Estate and three men got out, the Superintendent in uniform, the other two dressed formally in suits and ties, unusual in this part of the world. But the Superintendent had ordered this official appearance just as he had ordered the official police car, rather than the unmarked car usually driven by the detectives.

"The more intimidating it looks, the quicker they fall apart," he said to the detectives.

To finish off the scene, he put on his peaked cap that added quite a bit to his already imposing height. The senior officer led the way to Gerard's office and walked in without knocking.

Gerard was sitting behind his desk reading a newspaper, a mug of coffee by the side. His face registered complete astonishment and possibly some fear at this invasion, his mouth fell open and he reached for the mug of coffee. The Superintendent was highly experienced and he quickly spotted the trembling in Gerard's hands.

Without asking, the three men took chairs across the desk from Gerard.

"Are you aware that Max Bernard has returned?" said the Superintendent, watching the man carefully.

Gerard's face went white and now the expression was all fear. He said nothing.

"It's a month ahead of schedule, but as you may know, the flooding up in the Congo caused some serious traffic problems and he returned early. Mr Bernard has been giving us a lot of information about his travels," continued the officer. "It seems he hadn't just upped and left as we all had assumed, but had gone on a pre-arranged trip of some duration with his lady, one Elise Pelletier. Had you met Ms Pelletier?"

His mouth still open, Gerard shook his head.

"That's odd," said the officer. "Because Max said otherwise and in fact she was with him when he gave you some letters to post to Gary's family in the Seychelles. Do you remember being given those letters, Mr Gerard?"

"Of course, and I..." Gerard's voice was a croak. He took a sip from his coffee mug and tried again. "I posted them off a few days after they'd left, just as Max told me to."

"And yet none of them ever arrived. Are you quite certain you posted them?"

Gerard nodded, the tension in him radiating into the room.

"You see, Mr Gerard, here's what we've been thinking. If those letters were not posted and so never arrived, and Max was away for all the time you knew he would be, it would be simple to suggest to everybody that he'd gone missing. And that would give you time to do some financial fiddling with the company accounts, wouldn't it?"

Gerard could only shake his head, his face still ashen.

The Superintendent turned to one of the other two men and nodded. The detective reached into his inside jacket pocket and extracted an envelope, handing it to the officer.

"What made us think even more was that when we got a court order to examine the company accounts, we found significant sums had been transferred to an account in your name. Now why would you have done that?"

Gerard seemed frozen.

The Superintendent slid the envelope across the desk.

"That's the court order which is also a search warrant for these premises, Mr Gerard. So would you mind opening the safe?"

Like a sleepwalker, Gerard stood up and went to the safe, turned the dials and stood back. One of the detectives knelt by the door and started sifting through the few documents that were in there. The other detective began examining the documents on Gerard's desk and then all the books in the small bookshelf against one wall, taking out each one in turn and shuffling through the pages.

The Superintendent sat quietly, seemingly lost in thought.

"Sir!" The man at the safe turned back, holding a packet of envelopes which he handed to the officer. The Superintendent looked briefly at the addresses.

"Well now," he said. "One to Gary's mother, one to Gary, one to each of Gary's siblings. Looks like you've been a trifle careless, Mr Gerard."

"Well, hello!" said the second detective at the bookshelf as a coloured document fell out of one of the books. The oblong, colourful leaflet was an airline ticket. The detective picked it up and passed it to the officer who opened it up.

"Well now, look here," he said in pretend surprise. "An airline ticket from Nairobi for a Mr Francis Gerard, flying to London... and next week, too! Looks like we got here just in time, eh?"

He looked at Gerard and gave a wide smile.

"You're nicked, mate," he said. "Let's go."

Gary's father suffered greatly from the loss of his son and although he later married Elise and lived happily with her for the rest of his life, there was always a streak of sadness in him. The funeral was hailed as one of the largest ever held in Mombasa, attended by well over three hundred mourners. His pall-bearers were his four trusted Askaries, headed by Sergeant Thom and the Captain.

Part of the Captain's eulogy read, *"He entered and left our lives at sunrise."*

Karen was given special leave from work, and spent a lot of time at her beach house. She received counselling from her department but she and Anthony's wife who was very fond of Gary grieved for a long time.

A few months later, she flew to the Seychelles to meet Gary's family and kept in close contact. She devoted her entire time to her work and the memory of the love of her life.

*** The End ***

www.ingramcontent.com/pod-product-compliance
Lightning Source LLC
Chambersburg PA
CBHW071301250626
47159CB00004B/1255